A former Hollywood studio executive who gladly traded in her high heels and corner office for yoga pants and the local coffee shop, **Susannah Erwin** loves writing about ambitious, strong-willed people who can't help falling in love— whether they want to or not. Her first novel won the Golden Heart® Award from Romance Writers of America, and she is hard at work in her Northern California home on her next. She would be over the moon if you signed up for her newsletter via www.susannaherwin.com.

Who's the Boss Now?

SUSANNAH ERWIN

MILLS & BOON

First published in Great Britain 2021
by Mills & Boon, an imprint of HarperCollins*Publishers* Ltd,
1 London Bridge Street, London, SE1 9GF

www.harpercollins.co.uk

HarperCollins*Publishers*
1st Floor, Watermarque Building,
Ringsend Road, Dublin 4, Ireland

Large Print edition 2021

Who's the Boss Now? © 2021 Susannah Erwin

ISBN: 978-0-263-29321-0

08/21

MIX
Paper from
responsible sources
FSC
www.fsc.org
FSC™ C007454

This book is produced from independently certified
FSC™ paper to ensure responsible forest management.
For more information visit www.harpercollins.co.uk/green.

Printed and bound in Great Britain
by CPI Group (UK) Ltd, Croydon, CR0 4YY

For Nia, Isabel and Marie—
the best critique group
(and group of friends) a writer can have!

One

Breaking into the owner's private wine cellar at St. Isadore Winery was easy. The side door at the rear of the house stuck a little from disuse, but it led directly to the service stairs and Marguerite Delacroix's destination several flights below. Getting out, on the other hand...

Marguerite tried to lift the two full cases of wine at her feet and gave up, rubbing her aching arms as she considered the best way to make a quick exit. What had seemed like an excellent plan at 11:00 p.m. over a bottle—or two—of Carménère shared with her best friend, Aracely Contreras, turned out to have several flaws in its execution at one in the morning. To start, the bottles were heavy. Too heavy to carry up the stairs except a few at a time, which would take the rest of the night.

She held up her phone, with the flash-light app on, and did a slow, albeit unsteady, 360-degree pirouette, shining the light around the dark, chilly cellar with its dozens of wine racks lining the walls. But this just confirmed what she already knew. Her only other option was the elevator, but it was riskier.

She sighed. Of course, this wasn't going to be simple. Things never were at St. Isadore.

Marguerite grew up on stories about the fabled exploits of her Delacroix ancestors, legendary for their winemaking prowess. She was descended from the branch of the family that immigrated to California during the gold rush, producing wine for the state's fast-grow-ing population. One vineyard turned into five and St. Isadore was established shortly after, built to resemble a Loire Valley castle. Now it was one of the few remaining original win-eries in Napa.

The winery had survived the phylloxera virus, which had destroyed most of Napa's grapevines by the turn of the last century, and sailed through Prohibition thanks to savvy packaging and not a little smuggling. However, St. Isadore had almost gone under when two brothers inherited the estate after World War II and fought bitterly over how to run the business. Eventually, one brother had kept control of the winery while the other took the vineyards to manage for himself.

The two branches of the family had remained at odds until Marguerite's father, who had inherited the vineyards and then sold them ten years ago to the late Linus Chappell, who owned the winery. Marguerite had begged her parents to keep the land until she could take over its management, but neither of her parents had much interest in viticulture, and early retirement in Arizona had beckoned. She'd returned home after her junior year at UC Davis to find that the vineyards, for the first time in their history, no longer had an owner named Delacroix.

But even a reunited estate hadn't restored St. Isadore to its former glory. The more Northern California's wine country thrived off increased tourism and demand for its wines, the further St. Isadore seemed to fall behind.

New equipment did on occasion make its way into the winery, but the elevator in the cellar dated to the mid-1930s. It was as beautiful in its art deco detail as it was rickety and noisy. The engine room was underneath the owner's living quarters and could be heard—and felt—through several floors and walls. The family liked it that way. It served as another control on who accessed their private stash of rare and experimental wines and when.

At least the elevator was reliable; Marguerite knew from long experience. Besides, who was around to hear her use it? Linus had died six months ago without a will, and his entire estate had gone to his closest relatives, two great-nephews who'd immediately put the winery and its vineyards on the market. The sale of St. Isadore to a Silicon Valley tech CEO had been completed last week, and according to local gossip, he hadn't taken possession yet. And the local gossips would know. He was an object of intense interest, not the least because he was reputed to be ridiculously good-looking and single.

But the detail most important to Marguerite was when escrow closed, the security guards the great-nephews had installed disappeared. Which left her this one small window of opportunity.

She propped open the elevator's wooden outer door with a nearby wedge, then pulled back the ornate steel security gate and began loading wine bottles into the small cab. This was probably the last time she would set foot in the cellar. St. Isadore was targeted to be torn down and turned into a luxury housing development, if the rumors were correct.

Her breath caught in renewed pain at the thought.

But she could save the wine. *Her* wine. Wine that she hoped would be the first step to restoring the Delacroix name to winemaking prominence. Most of it was locked up in the winery and inaccessible, but Linus had asked for a sample bottle from each batch to store in the owner's cellar. Now these bottles were all she had left after eight years. Eight years of putting her whole heart into working for Linus because they had a handshake deal: he would pay her fifteen percent of her negotiated salary. The other eighty-five percent went toward buying back the original vineyard that started it all, with its grapes to be made into wine by her and sold by St. Isadore. She would not let the Delacroix name down.

And she had come so close! She'd finished paying off the vineyard on her last birthday, of all dates, and Linus had promised to transfer the deed. But then a stroke had suddenly taken his life. After his funeral the leatherbound ledger he'd used to record her steady progression toward ownership was nowhere to be found. When she'd tried to negotiate for the vineyard with Linus's great-nephews, they'd laughed in her face before calling the sheriff to remove her from the property.

The wine she'd made was all she had left and she'd be damned if she let it rot in the owner's cellar or worse, be destroyed. She gathered up the last bottle. Beads of sweat formed on her brow despite the cold of the cellar, and she brushed them away with a swipe of her arm, the scent of old, spilled wine and damp stone clinging to the sleeve of her loose T-shirt. Dust covered her hands, and she wiped them on her jeans before pushing the button for the ground floor. From there, it would be a short walk to the main entrance. Aracely was somewhere nearby, waiting for Marguerite's call. Together they would load the wine into Aracely's SUV and then make their getaway.

But to what? The only life Marguerite knew was here, at St. Isadore. All she'd ever wanted was to remain here. And she'd thought her agreement with Linus meant she would be able to stay forever.

Marguerite blinked back tears. No matter how much pain St. Isadore had caused her, it was home. And now the new tech-CEO owner would destroy it.

Evan Fletcher rubbed his closed eyes. It didn't help. When he opened them again, the numbers on his laptop screen remained the same: dismal.

When he first authorized his business manager to buy St. Isadore lock, stock and multiple barrels of wine, he had been pleased to learn not only was the winery fully equipped but the owner's residence came furnished. Then he arrived a few hours ago, finally able to inspect his purchase for himself, and learned that the photos so beautifully shot in the golden sunlight hid a myriad of imperfections and outright damage. But St. Isadore was still a working business and thus perfect for his needs. The rest was cosmetic.

"I'd love to say I told you so, but not only is it late, I want to keep you as a client," said his business manager from the speaker on Evan's phone, followed by an audible yawn.

"It's okay, Pia. Rub it in all you want. It's the least I deserve after calling at this hour. I thought I'd be leaving a voice mail."

"I've learned if I don't pick up the phone when I see your number, by the time I call back you've dug an even bigger hole—like making an offer on a winery sight unseen."

"Next time I'll call during business hours. This was the first quiet moment I had today, between getting things settled here and a new crisis erupting at work."

"I thought things were calming down on that front."

"Define calm." Evan was the CEO and founder of Medevco, a fast-growing tech start-up in artificial intelligence-based medical devices that had hit a billion-dollar valuation a year ago, making it what Silicon Valley insiders liked to a call a "unicorn" because such companies were rare and exciting. But with growth came growing pains. Expensive ones. And lots of them.

He shook his head to clear it. One potential disaster at a time. Right now, the winery took precedence. "Thanks for going through the St. Isadore numbers with me. And tell me how to best apologize to Luisa for keeping you so late."

Pia laughed. "Like time has any meaning since the baby arrived. And no need to apologize. She'll thank you because I'll be up for the two a.m. feeding and she can sleep. But if you truly feel bad, send us a case of Chardonnay…but maybe from another winery."

"Ha ha," Evan deadpanned. "You'll see. By this time next year, you'll be begging me for a case of St. Isadore's finest."

"This isn't a tech company. It's a completely different industry, and you purchased a small winery that didn't produce up to its capacity even before the senior staff left. You can't expect your usual Midas touch to kick in."

"That sounds like a challenge."

"Depends on how high your expectations are. And knowing you, they're stratospheric."

Evan scratched the back of his head but stayed silent. New mothers didn't need additional stress.

"I heard that," Pia said.

"Heard what?"

"The sound of you keeping something from me."

"The Global Leader Summit is being held in Napa this summer."

Pia's exhale was audible through the speaker. "Please don't tell me what you're about to tell me."

"The organizers heard I was purchasing a winery and asked if I would be interested in hosting the kickoff social event. Of course, I said yes."

Pia groaned. "Evan, those are some of the world's most important business leaders—"

"It'll be fine."

"This has nothing to do with Angus Horne

blowing off your phone calls, does it? He always attends the summit. And he's quite the wine connoisseur."

Evan laughed. "Would I buy an entire winery and the corresponding estate simply to corner an investor for Medevco?"

Pia scoffed, "You'd buy the moon if you thought it would give you quality face time with Horne to work your magic. You forget, I watch over your accounts when you refuse to. Bottom line is this, Evan. With so much of your capital tied up in Medevco, the winery purchase put a strain on your liquid assets."

"The winery is revenue producing."

He heard her fingers tapping on her keyboard. "Revenue but not necessarily profit. And you'll need to make several capital investments in the property. You can run it at a loss for a year without giving me gray hairs."

"I'll do my best." He'd hired Pia as his business manager for her cautious approach. But he hadn't sold three companies before the age of thirty, then founded and become CEO of Medevco, without having the utmost confidence in his judgment and skills. Pia might call it his Midas touch, but he preferred to think of it as creative risk-taking combined with a ruthless ability to cut his losses. "Thanks again. And hey, try to get a nap in before the kid wakes up."

He disconnected the call and leaned back in his chair. At least the place was clean, the shower had plenty of hot water—his hair was still slightly damp from the one he'd taken before calling Pia back—and the new beds had been delivered that evening and made up with fresh linens.

He rose and stretched, intending to discover if the mattress was as comfortable as it looked, and a low rumbling shook the scuffed parquet floor under his feet. "What the—?"

His gaze whipped around the room. Years of living in California with the ever-present possibility of earthquakes had taught him how to seek the safest spot to wait out the tremors. But the rumbling didn't get worse, nor did it stop. It stayed a steady hum. A machine-generated hum.

Of course. The elevator. The one that led to the private cellars built deep underground. His pulse rate fell.

Then it sped up again. He was the only person awake in the house. The other occupant had gone to bed several hours ago.

He didn't believe in ghosts, despite the furniture in the residence resembling rejects from Disneyland's Haunted Mansion. But the elevator dated well into the last century. It was probably malfunctioning.

He sighed. Better check it out. The last thing he needed was a fire caused by faulty wiring.

He passed by the arched entrance to the kitchen on his way to investigate. Through the doorway, he spotted a heavy cast-iron frying pan sitting on top of the ancient stove. He grabbed it.

Just in case he was wrong about ghosts. And they came armed.

The elevator ground to a halt. Marguerite hit the stop button and pulled back the steel gate. Bending down, she picked up and cradled three bottles in her arms, then used her back to push open the wooden door. Mission accomplished. And no one would ever know she'd been there. She straightened up and turned around—

—and came face-to-face with a half-dressed man, his chest as bare as his feet, the cast-iron skillet in his hands aimed squarely at her head.

She screamed. Two of the bottles slid out of her arms. They landed with a thud on the elevator cab's worn linoleum floor. Pure instinct took over, her mind swallowed by a cloud of fear and panic. She grasped the third bottle by the neck, then pulled it back over her right shoulder like an extremely short baseball bat.

And swung.

The man brought the pan up to cover his face. The bottle met the heavy cast iron. The air rang with the cracking of glass.

The cool liquid cascading over Marguerite's hands caused her brain to come back online. She blinked in rapid succession, her adrenaline still surging. "Oh, no. Oh, no no *no*."

What was she doing? All her hard work, her last connection to St. Isadore, was now a spreading stain on the floor. She immediately brought the bottle to a vertical position, the cork end pointed at the floor. It was hard to tell in the darkened foyer, but it looked like she had lost a third of the wine.

She could save the rest. Maybe. Her mind raced, seeking options.

The man lowered the cast-iron skillet, letting it fall to his side. She had been so focused on the bottle, she'd almost forgotten she wasn't alone.

They stared at each other for a heartbeat, their chests rising and falling almost in unison. So this was the ridiculously handsome new owner. She recognized the square jaw with the perpetual five-o'clock shadow, the thick dark brows set atop a piercing gaze from news stories on the internet. But neither the photos nor the gossip had conveyed the breadth of his shoulders, the way he exuded power and strength, despite being clad in only low-slung sweatpants that draped off narrow hips.

And she was the interloper here, not him. "Are you going to use that thing?" she croaked, pointing at the pan.

He shook his head, his mouth working for a few beats. "What the *hell*?" exploded from his lips. "Who the—?"

"I can explain." He was furious. Deservedly so. But she had a bigger concern at the moment. "Right now, I need a new bottle. A container. Something." She started to push past him, the bottle cradled against her.

He caught her arm with his left hand. His grip was solid and warm after the chill of the cellar. Wine splashed on her shirt, and her breath caught. She wouldn't be able to break free. Not without losing what wine remained—and leaving behind all her other bottles.

"No, you don't," he growled. "Explain now."

"Let me go and I will."

His eyebrows shot toward his hairline. "Let you— Lady, you tried to clobber me!"

"You threatened me first!" With her chin, she indicated the frying pan in his right hand. "And you're right. I'm sorry. But you scared me."

"You're breaking into my house!"

"Technically, I'm about to leave your house. Which I'm still happy to do. But please. I need something to hold the wine." She met his gaze for the first time. His eyes glittered in the dim light. She took in a gulp of air. "Please."

His frown deepened, but his hold on her sleeve loosened enough for her to twist and feint right before dodging around him to the left, to find the door—wallpapered to blend in with the rest of the wall—that led to the service corridor, and beyond it, the kitchen. There had to be something she could use in there.

The heat of his fingers continued to linger on her skin.

Evan blinked. Did the thief...disappear into the wall? What the *hell*?

He glanced at the bottles still in the elevator. They didn't have labels. Instead, it looked like someone had scrawled notes on the glass with a paint pen.

That made no sense at all. The owner's cellar contained rare and very valuable wine. A thief out to make a profit would have gone for the bottles most likely to fetch a high price on the market. What was his intruder up to?

He explored the area of the wall where she had disappeared and discovered the door, left slightly ajar. A vague memory surfaced of the agent who had represented the estate talking enthusiastically about secret passageways. Evan thought it had been real estate hype, an attempt to upsell a back stairway or an attic crawl space. But no. The house did indeed come with hidden entrances and hallways. And his late-night guest knew about them.

He paused to listen, then followed the faint sound of rustling to another door. Pushing it open, he discovered he was back in the kitchen, a cavernous space with appliances that would be right at home in a 1950s sit-com. Two cabinets had their doors flung open, while a wine bottle sat propped upside down in the dish rack next to the stainless steel sink.

The thief was rummaging through a third cabinet. She threw him a glance over her shoulder. "Where are the carafes?" she asked. "Linus kept them here. Did you move them?"

Evan patted the pockets of his sweatpants for his phone, intending to call the authorities and hold her there until they arrived. However, his pockets were empty. He must have left his phone in the other room. "Talk. Who are you? What are you doing here?"

She turned to face him. He had his first good look at her in the bright glare of the overhead lights. Dark hair, more raven than chestnut, had been twisted into a bun at the top of her head, but several locks had escaped, the wavy tendrils sticking out every which way. Her skin was pale, almost translucent in contrast to the black T-shirt and dark skinny jeans she wore. Those jeans outlined long, slender legs that led to gently curved hips, but her loose-fitting top concealed the rest of her curves. He dragged his gaze back up to her face. The freezing glare he received informed him he had been caught looking. "Carafes?" she repeated.

"You don't seem to understand who I am or how much trouble you're in. I ask the questions."

Her mouth twisted. "Oh, I understand. You're St. Isadore's new owner. The tech guy. The entire valley has been wondering when you would arrive, although obviously, I didn't think you'd moved in yet. In fact, I would've put money down that you wouldn't move in at all. So, carafes. Are they in the butler's pantry?"

He shook his head, confused, but he'd puzzle her words out later. "I didn't put anything anywhere. I've barely set foot in this room." She glanced at the iron skillet still loosely held in his right hand and raised an eyebrow. He put the pan back on the blackened burner on top of the antique stove. He didn't get the feeling from her he would require it. "Except to get this. You, however, seem to know the place well. Who are you?"

"Maybe if you examined the kitchen as thoroughly as you check out women's bodies, you'd know where things are." Her tone was light as she continued searching the cabinet, but she held her head as if she were a monarch giving the annual address to the kingdom's subjects.

"Just ensuring I can give the authorities an accurate description of who broke into my home."

"I didn't break in. I have a key." She opened another door. "Most people change the locks when they move into a new place, you know."

She had a key? He added that piece of information to his mental catalog of surprising things he'd learned about his thief. "You don't have an invitation. That makes it a break-in."

"In California, I believe that makes it trespassing." She took out a small plastic water pitcher, scratched and discolored from years of use. "May I borrow this, please?"

He narrowed his gaze. "I'm not a lawyer, but if *Law and Order* reruns have taught me anything, it's only trespassing—which is still a misdemeanor—if you don't intend to commit a crime. The wine stacked in my elevator says otherwise."

She crossed the kitchen and started to pull out cabinet drawers, one after the other. Have you seen—aha!" She pulled out a corkscrew. "I'm not committing a crime. Well, okay, I'll agree I am trespassing. But not stealing." Her voice trailed off as she lifted the upside-down wine bottle from where it rested in the dish rack to inspect it. "At least it was a clean crack, which is weird because I doubt I hit the pan hard enough to cause one." She poured the contents into the pitcher and then sighed, her shoulders falling. "There. I wish the wine could age more, but at least I can taste it."

Then she turned to face him. "Thank you for not calling the sheriff. And for your patience. I owe you an explanation—"

Blue-and-red revolving lights appeared, shining through the kitchen window to cast multicolored shadows. The sound of slamming car doors accompanied them. She raised her eyebrows. "I guess you did call them."

Evan shook his head. What the hell? "I don't have my phone on me." He pointed at her. "Stay here. I want your story."

He made his way to the front entrance, flicked on the lights and opened one of the heavy wooden doors. The chilled January night air rushed in, but his focus was on the sheriff's car parked in the circular gravel driveway with its lights still flashing. Two men stood by the car, speaking to each other. "Evening," Evan called out, although it was more like early morning. "What's the trouble, deputies?"

The taller and stockier of the two men straightened up. "No trouble. Sorry to disturb you."

The shorter, leaner man strode toward the

door. As he came closer, Evan could make out his face. His heart sank past his stomach.

"Nico."

His younger brother pushed past him without a word. Evan turned to the sheriff. "What did he do?"

"Who, Nico? Oh, he's not in trouble. But he was a passenger in a car pulled over because the driver was under the influence. Now, your brother is sober, but he doesn't have a valid driver's license and therefore couldn't take over the operation of the vehicle. I was finished with my shift, so I offered to give him a ride here."

"With flashing lights?" Adrenaline still thumped in Evan's veins. The night just kept getting more surreal.

The sheriff ignored his question and waved instead. "Hey, Marguerite."

"Hello, Deputy Franks."

Evan turned to see the thief standing behind him, lit by the ornate wrought iron chandelier hanging in the foyer.

"Didn't think you still lived here," the sheriff said.

The thief—Marguerite, Evan mentally corrected himself—shot Evan a glance. When he didn't speak, she took a deep breath. "I don't."

The sheriff's gaze ping-ponged between Evan and Marguerite, and Evan remembered for the first time since finding his thief that he was wearing only a pair of sweatpants. Then the sheriff nodded. "All right. Well. I should get going."

"Thanks for bringing Nico home." Evan shut the front door and turned to Marguerite. "I still want your story. First I have to find my brother."

"He's in the kitchen," she said. "He seems angry. That's why I came to find you."

"Nico is always angry," Evan muttered.

"Why didn't you tell the sheriff you caught me trespassing?" She cocked her head. More dark locks fell from her messy bun to frame her high cheekbones.

Evan didn't answer. He wasn't sure if he had an answer. "My brother, then you," he repeated and motioned for her to lead the way.

Nico sat at the wide oak table that occupied one end of the kitchen. He had a loaf of bread and a mammoth jar of peanut butter by one elbow, and he was chugging from—

"Oh, no," Marguerite exclaimed. She extricated the pitcher from Nico's grasp. Only a few drops remained. If Nico wasn't drunk when he got here, he was now doing his best to remedy that.

That was the last straw for a night that contained more straw than a haystack. Evan slammed his palms down on the table. Nico and Marguerite both raised startled gazes to meet his. "Start talking." He pointed at Nico. "You first. You went to bed hours ago."

"I changed my mind," Nico said, his tone as flat as the piece of bread he was spreading with peanut butter. A shock of light brown hair fell across his forehead and hid his eyes, but Evan knew Nico's gaze would be just as expressionless. "A girl I met earlier called and said she and her friends were going out and she'd come get me. You were in the shower."

"You need to tell me."

"I know you forget, but I'm twenty-one years old. So, no, I don't." Nico bit into his sandwich. "But I texted you when the sheriff pulled us over. Thanks for picking me up, by the way. Having the sheriff drive me back here wasn't at all humiliating."

"I—" Damn it. His phone was in the living room. And he hadn't looked at his messages since he first sat down to go through paperwork four hours ago. It felt like a century had passed. "We're not talking about me," he finally said. "We're talking about you."

Nico's response was to take another bite out of his sandwich. "Who's she?" he asked, jerking a thumb at Marguerite.

"Oh, no," Marguerite said again, with an entirely different intonation. She clutched the water pitcher to her chest. "I'm not a part of this. I'll grab my things and go."

"Do 'your things' include the multiple bottles of wine you're stealing?" Evan asked.

"More wine?" Nico perked up. "If it's what I was drinking, it's excellent."

"Really?" Marguerite smiled, the first real smile Evan had seen from her. And it was… amazing. He'd noted she had expressive eyes, the dark blue of an evening sky. But when she smiled, they glowed, making her appear lit from within. "That bottle was pretty young."

"Tasted great to me." Nico carried his plate to the sink.

"Thanks." Marguerite sniffed what remained in the water pitcher. "But a wine expert would say—"

"Too much tannin, so yeah, it would benefit from more aging. But the flavors were nicely balanced. Anyway, good night." Nico left the kitchen without a backward glance.

"Hey, we're not done—" Evan called after him, but Marguerite's hand on his arm caused the rest of his words to die in his throat. He glanced down at where her slender fingers rested on his bare bicep.

Pink colored her cheeks. She took her hand away and stepped to the sink where she washed out the water pitcher. "Let him go. He was spoiling for a fight, but now he's thrilled he scored a point off me. Allow him his victory."

Evan still felt the pressure of her touch. "You're not only a thief, you're a psychologist? Multitalented."

Her color deepened and she held her chin up. "I'm neither. I'm a winemaker. And I was once his age." Her tone implied that Evan must not remember what it was like to be a young adult.

She was right. He didn't. Because when he was Nico's age, he was running his first company. Nor did he need to be reminded by a thief of the chasm between Nico and him, no matter how intriguing he found her. "My brother isn't your concern."

She raised her eyebrows. "Okay. So, like I said, let me get my things—"

"You still owe me your story. Let me guess—you say you're a winemaker, so you made the wine you're steal—"

"*Not* stealing."

"Liberating, then." He made air quotes with his fingers. "But I don't remember a Marguerite listed among St. Isadore's key staff. I thought the head winemaker was a Calvin or a Cassian or a—"

"Casper. Casper Vos. He's at Dellavina Cellars now." Steel shutters slammed down behind her eyes, turning her gaze opaque.

Evan regarded her. "You don't seem to like him."

"Most of St. Isadore's staff is now gone," she said, ignoring his comment.

"I see that for myself."

"They started to leave even before Linus had his stroke. Might not be a bad thing to have to start over. Loyalty wasn't their strong suit." A bitter breeze danced through her words.

He leaned against the table. "Except for you, I take it. What was your role at St. Isadore?"

She sighed. "That's a complicated question."

He waved his hand at the dark windows. "There are a few hours left before sunrise."

She opened her mouth—

The lights overhead winked and went out. The room plunged into darkness.

Two

Marguerite stood still, allowing her eyes to adjust to the sudden change. But apparently her companion had other ideas. She heard a thump and a crash, followed by several muttered words she couldn't quite make out, but she was sure most of them had four letters. "You okay?" she said.

"This damn night" was the response. "What the hell is happening now?"

Marguerite chuckled. She couldn't help it, even though her heart still pounded painfully from being caught trying to sneak away with her wine. Her pulse had started racing from the moment the bottom of the bottle had hit the frying pan and now continued to act as if she were competing in the last leg of a triathlon.

Or at least that's why she told herself her heart was pumping overtime. It had nothing to do with the fact Evan Fletcher wore nothing but sweatpants, which constantly threatened to fall off his narrow hips. She was almost glad the lights were off so she wouldn't have to work so hard to keep her eyes from lingering on his impressive pecs and the wall of abdominal muscles below.

"The previous owner's memory started to slip toward the end. He was afraid he'd forget to turn off lights and run up the electricity bill, so every room is on a timer."

"At two a.m.?" He sounded both put out and disbelieving.

"He was a night owl. I'll get them back on."

"I can turn on my own lights," he muttered, followed by the scrape of furniture against the floor and another thud. A loud thud.

Marguerite gasped. It was bad enough the sheriff had seen her at St. Isadore late at night. If he had to come back because the new owner was hurt while she was on the premises…it would not do her reputation, already tattered after her confrontation with Linus's nephews, any favors. As it was, she could already hear tomorrow's gossip leapfrogging from breakfast table to luncheon counter thanks to Deputy Franks spotting her with a half-dressed Evan tonight.

She struggled to distinguish shape from shadow in the dark, but Evan had to be near the kitchen table. She moved quickly—only to trip over what in hindsight she realized were his bare feet. She stumbled and went down, her hands stopping her fall. "Ow!"

"That hurt, damn it," came the grumpy voice from her left.

"Are you okay? What happened?"

"Chair. Nico didn't push it in."

He sounded so disgruntled, she had to laugh. "No broken bones, I take it."

"Just my broken dignity. What little remained. You okay? Sounded like you went down harder than me."

Her wrists stung from taking the brunt of her fall. She ran a quick check of the rest of her body. Feeling the firm hardness of his thigh under her left calf, she realized her legs were entwined with his. She quickly untangled herself. "Um. No. More shocked by finding myself on the floor than hurt."

He gathered himself together and stood. Now that her eyes had adjusted to the dark, she could see him extending a hand to her. "Here, let me help you."

She took it. His palm was warm, his grip tight and reassuring. She scrambled to her feet, but when she put weight on her right ankle, it was agony. "Ouch!"

He appeared at her side, encouraging her to lean on him. "Sprain or something worse?"

She shook her head. "Twisted. It will be okay." She tried to move away from his side but couldn't put weight on her foot.

"C'mon." He tugged her down to sit beside him. "My shins are going to be black-and-blue from fighting with the chair. And I hit my knee when I fell, so I'm not up to carrying you at the moment. May I offer you some floor?"

Not a bad offer; the hardwood was cool but rather comfortable. She picked a spot that kept her legs from touching his and propped her back against one of the cabinets. After withdrawing her hand from his, she instantly regretted the loss of his warmth.

The room was dark and still. Shadows pressed in, but they created a cocoon, wrapping the two of them together against the outside world. Without sight, her other senses sharpened. Her ears picked up his soft breaths. And her nose, trained to distinguish slight variations in wine aromas, inhaled lemongrass and basil and something else she could define as only warm, clean skin. Her pulse thudded in her veins.

All she had to do was move her hand slightly to the left and it would brush his, perhaps be enveloped again in his comforting strength. And maybe he would use that excuse to pull her closer and she could let her fingers trace in the dark what she had been afraid to explore with her gaze in the light: the smooth bronzed skin over defined biceps, the dark hair dusting his chest before it narrowed to a trail that disappeared below the drawstring of his sweatpants...

He cleared his throat, and her mind jumped back to reality. "That makes three surprises about this place so far," he said. "Four, if I count you. The elevator works despite looking like a museum piece, the secret hallway isn't real estate fiction, and the lights turn off on their own. And it's only my first night."

"That's St. Isadore. I learned something new every day. No matter how long I worked here."

He turned toward her, but she couldn't read his expression in the dim light. "What did you do here anyway? Especially if Custer was the winemaker."

She let out a mirthless laugh. "Casper. Like I said, it's complicated."

"Great. You owe me a story, might as well be a good one."

She huffed. "Fine." But there was no need to go into the details with him. "I was Linus's live-in personal assistant. Jill-of-all-trades, I suppose you could call me. As long as I did what he needed me to do, my time was my own, and I spent it making wine. The previous winemaker agreed to mentor me—" She was proud her voice didn't crack. Casper's abrupt departure for one of the premier wineries in the country accompanied by his curt dismissal of her talent still smarted "—and

I experimented on my own with blends and methods."

"If you're a winemaker, why be a personal assistant? Find a job making wine."

She pressed her lips together. Her reasons for being at St. Isadore were personal and tangled and messy—although not as personal and tangled and messy as the gossip spread by others. Including the gossip spread by Casper, who ensured her reputation as an innovative winemaker was ruined. And from what she knew of Evan Fletcher, he would have zero idea why she cared so much.

She settled on: "The grapes aren't the same somewhere else." She heard his intake of breath as he prepared to speak, and she cut him off. "Don't ever say that a grape is just a grape. Not around here."

She didn't need light to see his eye roll. "Despite what you're thinking, I'm not some dense tech guy. I was going to ask why St. Isadore's vines are so special. I own them, after all."

They're special because they're mine. But saying that out loud would take explanations about her tangled family history she didn't want to give, along with admitting how she allowed others to take advantage of her good faith. And she doubted he would be fobbed off with a few vague sentences. The tech guy definitely wasn't dense—well, except for maybe his muscles. "What makes them special? The terroir."

"The terror?"

She laughed. "You're kidding, right? You know what terroir is."

"Yes. A little. Actually, let's say no."

"Terroir is the concept that the specific conditions of where the grapes are grown—the soil, the wind, the sun, the elevation—affect the wine's flavor."

He nodded. "Terroir makes the vines unique."

She smiled. "Which means the wine made from them is unique. There's more to it, of course, but that's the nutshell." Then she sobered. "I guess this means the rumors are right."

"What rumors?"

"About you."

"Me? What are they saying?" Was it her imagination, or had he leaned closer to her? Then she felt his breath on her cheek and understood he was all too real. Pinpricks of awareness flared on her skin.

She swallowed. "Nothing, really. Nothing bad. They say you bought St. Isadore only to tear it down and sell it off piece by piece."

"*They*," he emphasized the word as he shifted away from her, "have no idea why I bought this place."

It was weird to miss someone's breath near your ear, right? But she did. "Why else would a superrich tech dude buy a winery that's seen better days? Unless maybe as a tax shelter. I'm not familiar with how those work. But either way, it's obvious you didn't buy St. Isadore because you have an affinity for viticulture. So why did you buy it?"

The brooding silence only increased the arctic temperature in the room. He finally spoke. "St. Isadore is a business. I buy and run businesses."

Her hands clenched and unclenched. "You plan to keep St. Isadore going as a winery? Produce wine? Distribute it? Not develop the land?"

"That's why I bought it. As a going business." He huffed. "If I can make it one."

Butterfly wings of hope fluttered in her chest. St. Isadore wouldn't be torn down. Its vineyards wouldn't be sold and destroyed.

Maybe the dream that had sustained her since childhood wasn't gone for good. Maybe she could save her family's legacy. Oh, Evan wouldn't agree to the same arrangement she'd had with Linus, nor would she dream of proposing it. She trusted Linus—wrongly, as it turned out—because he had been like a grandfather to her, and Evan…was anything but grandfatherly. And look how that had turned out. She'd worked her butt off and received little in tangible reward except for bottles of wine she had to sneak in and liberate.

Marguerite tried to search Evan's gaze. But despite her eyes having long ago adjusted to the lack of illumination, she couldn't read him. She stood up, using the cabinet handles and countertop as leverage, and walked-hopped across the kitchen to the far wall, where she located the switch. Bright, hot light bathed the room as she turned back to him.

He was blinking rapidly. "You could have warned me before you did that."

"Sorry. I will next time."

"Next time? Are you planning on making this a regular thing?"

She nodded. "You're going to hire me."

He blinked again, but she doubted the glare was the cause this time. "Excuse me?"

"You need me."

He ran his gaze up and down her figure, and his mouth curved into a teasing grin. "We just met. A little presumptuous, don't you think?"

She balled her hands on her hips. "You need me to help you bring St. Isadore back up to speed. You said it yourself—most of the staff is gone."

He narrowed his gaze. "I already have an assistant."

She smiled, a long, slow smile. "I'm not going to be your assistant. I'm going to be your winemaker."

This was the strangest night of Evan's life so far. And that included when an ex-girlfriend had persuaded him to attend a private séance at the Winchester Mystery House. The last few hours had delivered far more surprises than that evening had.

But it had also been one of the more intriguing nights of his life. And exciting, even though he didn't want to examine the physical side of his reaction to Marguerite too closely. Yes, he had a tendency to fall hard when dark eyes that spoke more eloquently than words ever could were involved. But this night, for all its surprises, made one thing clear: Pia wasn't wrong.

He was in uncharted waters. He might have bitten off more than even his vaunted business skills and reliable intuition could handle. And if he failed, his plan to solve Nico's problems would disappear down the drain like the remnants of Marguerite's wine.

But was Marguerite the life preserver he needed?

"First, you're a thief—" He held up his hand to stop the protest forming on her lips. Her plump, lush lips. "Fine. You weren't stealing. But you agreed you were trespassing."

"Because I thought you were going to tear down St. Isadore. Look, if I'm an actual thief, would I take the bottles worth gazillions of dollars that are sitting untouched in the cellar or the 'unmarked swill,' as you put it?"

He'd made the same point to himself earlier. "Then you said you were the personal assistant to the previous owner. But the business was about to go under. Why should I turn it over it you?" The one thing he did understand about wineries was the winemaker was a key role in its success or failure.

"It's true St. Isadore didn't live up to its potential. Linus didn't believe in introducing new technologies, no matter how hard we tried to change his mind. But I worked here for eight years. I know the winery. I know the vines. Above all, I know what St. Isadore is capable of becoming." She raised her eyebrows. "And in case you haven't noticed, you don't have anyone else."

"I can hire someone."

She shrugged. "You could. But they won't have my experience or specific knowledge of this place." She smiled, and he could swear the light in the kitchen increased by one hundred watts. "Besides, your brother likes my wine."

She probably meant the last as a joke, but it was a strong argument in her favor. Evan was still figuring out who Nico was, but he knew one thing: his brother was a wine savant, whether he came by it genetically or thanks to growing up with their Italian grandparents and their ever-present bottle of wine at the dinner table. Nico had a palate that sommeliers at Michelin-starred restaurants would envy.

And a chip on his shoulder big enough to be seen from the International Space Station, but Evan would find the key to removing it. Somehow.

His gut told him Marguerite wasn't lying. It was evident she cared about St. Isadore. She would be as invested in the winery's success as he was. And his instincts hadn't betrayed him yet. "As it so happens, I do need to hire someone—"

"At the going market rate. Benefits included. And a contract. A signed contract."

He bit back his smile. "You didn't let me finish. Yes, St. Isadore needs a winemaker. But I need someone to ensure the winery is able to hold a prestigious event in six months."

Her gaze narrowed. "Six months?"

"I'm hosting the opening kickoff for the Global Leader Summit here."

"Global Leader Summit…wait. I've heard of that. Isn't that where CEOs and world leaders get together for a week of secret meetings and when it's over, the public finds out Amazon agreed to buy Disney?"

"Amazon and Disney remain separate companies, but yes. The event will put St. Isadore on the map if it goes well."

She nodded. "And if it doesn't, you face-plant in front of some of the world's most powerful people."

Not that he would admit that. "So, if you want to stay at St. Isadore for longer than six months? Make sure the event is flawless."

Her chin jutted into the air. "Six months puts us before harvest. The winery has a bare-bones staff at the moment, so we need to hire more people immediately. At good salaries with excellent benefits. And if you want a flawless event, you need to hire a flawless event planner. Luckily, I know the best one in wine country."

"I believe in compensating my teams very well. But in return, the only acceptable outcome is success."

"*I* know what I'm doing." Besides, your

event will be a good dress rehearsal for the annual harvest dinner, which will make or break St. Isadore's reputation under your ownership."

"Harvest dinner?" He searched his memory of the buyer's paperwork and came up blank.

"It's a winery tradition, has been for over a century. Tickets go for hundreds of dollars. We debut the new wines and it's heavily covered by the industry press. You will definitely need someone who understands St. Isadore." She assessed him from under thick eyelashes and held out her right hand. "Deal?"

He closed the distance between them and shook. "Deal."

This close, he could see her eyes were several shades of blue, from almost navy on the rim to the color of afternoon sky nearer the pupil. She pushed a lock of hair off her cheek, and he caught the strawberry scent. This was either going to be one of the smartest hiring decisions he'd made or it might sink him. Personally.

"I guarantee you'll be pleased," she said. Was it his imagination or did she linger on the last word? A wicked light danced in her gaze as it met and held his. "Here's to a mutually successful outcome."

He wondered what it would be like to kiss her. To taste her mouth and see if wickedness had a flavor. Feel her open beneath him, inviting him in. See if her lips and tongue were as playful as the words they formed.

He owed a huge debt of gratitude to whoever first came up with sweatpants and made them loose enough to avoid possible embarrassment.

A cell phone rang and she jumped. He blinked, the sound dumping a bucket of cold water on his overheated imagination. "I… don't have my phone with me."

"It's mine." She pulled an older model cell from the back pocket of her jeans and glanced at the screen. "Oh, no. I can't believe I forgot." She answered the phone. "Hey, Aracely."

Whoever was on the other end was not happy. And did not let Marguerite get a word in. Evan walked to the sink, ostensibly to pour himself a glass a water. And to let the rest of him catch up with the change in the atmosphere. Yes, his libido wanted to kiss her.

But his intellect said he needed to employ her. And the two actions did not, would not mix.

Marguerite finished her conversation and hung up. "That's my ride. She'll be here in a few minutes." She put her phone away and turned to face him. "I'll see you first thing in the morning? Nine o'clock at the winery offices?"

"Make it noon. Get some sleep."

"Noon, it is." She hesitated for a second, then seemed to think better of what she was going to say. Instead, she gave him a half wave. "See you then." She ran-walked out of the kitchen, his gaze following her until she disappeared.

His instincts never failed him.

He only hoped it was his *business* instincts that had hired her, not something more primal.

Three

"If I were a ledger no one can find, where would I be?" Marguerite tapped her finger on her chin as she stood in the doorway of Linus's old office at the winery. Her gaze wandered over shelves that needing dusting and the collection of paperweights, still where Linus had left them, on top of the ornate mahogany desk. Marguerite had barely slept after she said goodbye to Evan the night before, so her vision was a bit blurry. But she didn't need it. She could describe every inch of the room in detail even if she wore a blindfold.

It was harder than she thought to cross the

threshold. Not that she thought she would find the ledger in the room. The last time she'd been in the office, it was to pack all the winery's business records under the watchful eyes of Linus's grand-nephews. The ledger had been missing then, although Marguerite had been too shell-shocked by grief to give it more than a cursory thought. Later, of course, she'd realized without it she had no proof of her deal with Linus.

Marguerite willed the moisture forming in her eyes to go away. She'd never known her grandparents, and Linus had been the closest thing to one she'd ever had. She still missed him. She probably always would. But he had also been her boss. And now his office was hers. She sat down in the immense leather chair behind the desk, ignoring the chill that climbed up her spine and settled on the back of her neck at hearing the upholstery creak, like it had all those times Linus had leaned forward to catch Marguerite's eye and solemnly impart a line of wisdom.

She shook her head. The office needed redecorating. The past would be the first thing to go.

"Good morning. The security guard said you were here."

She jumped and looked up. Evan stood in the doorway, leaning a shoulder against the jamb, his arms casually folded. She almost didn't recognize him, dressed in the Northern California business casual uniform of khakis and a button-down shirt. A part of her missed being able to feast her eyes on his rather glorious pecs and well-defined abs, but the crisp dark blue shirt provided its own visual pleasures, contrasting with his tanned skin and wavy dark hair.

Any lack of sleep from last night's encounter didn't show on his face, making Marguerite all too aware of her own tired appearance. His smile was warm, reminding her of how much she'd wanted to flirt with him the night before and how she had failed at it—luckily. Workplace romances were Not a Good Thing.

She offered a quick prayer of gratitude that she'd remembered to put on mascara before leaving for the winery.

"Good morning," she responded. "I know we said noon, but I thought I'd arrive a little early."

"Now works better for me, if it's okay with you?" At her nod, he crossed the room and placed a manila folder on her desk. "Here's the employment contract you asked for."

"My contract? Don't I get to negotiate my own—" She took the document out of the folder and glanced at the top page. A dollar sign followed by a very large number leaped out at her. "Oh."

"We can renegotiate if you like," he said with a straight face, but a glint in his eye betrayed his humor.

She blinked several times. No, she wasn't imagining the number. "I'm sure you don't often hear these words, but this is too much. I said I wanted the going market rate. This is at least twice that."

He sat down in the guest chair opposite her desk, his broad frame filling it completely. Evan owned his surroundings with a breezy confidence that made him even more attractive—and when he smiled at her, her stomach squeezed in the most delicious way. "Are you saying your time and effort aren't valuable?"

"No, I—" She stopped and took a deep breath, getting her unruly feelings under control. "You just met me. I have yet to work one day for you. Why are you paying me this much?"

He shrugged. "I asked around first thing this morning. Everyone I spoke to said you were the one who kept St. Isadore running these past years. I'm still curious why you were only the assistant, however."

Because that was the bargain. "Only the assistant?" She stared over the top of the document at him. "Does your assistant know you have so little regard for the role?"

"I promote mine," he responded. "I don't keep them in what amounts to indentured servitude. I looked up your salary, and you were badly underpaid. Think of this as the back pay you're due"

"There are other forms of compensation besides money."

He shook his head. "In my experience? Not really."

She opened her mouth to defend Linus by explaining their agreement. Then she closed her lips with a snap. She'd just met Evan, but it was clear he dealt in hard logic and cold cash. Telling him might make him doubt her business skills at best. At worst, he could have her thrown her off the premises, like Linus's grand-nephews had when she told them. And Evan had even more cause to bar her from St. Isadore, since he'd caught her red-handed breaking into the owner's residence.

She tapped the contract. "I see that. So there must be a catch somewhere..." She read on. "Ah. Found it. I see there's a performance review at six months and I can be terminated at will without cause until then."

"The Global Leader Summit event, as we discussed last night. I told you I cut losses fast and early."

She waved off his concern. "Don't worry, your rich friends will be impressed. Is that all it will take to pass the performance review? A successful event? It's a pretty simple ask."

He gave her a one-shouldered shrug. "I'm a simple man with simple wants."

"That's not what you said last night. I highly doubt there's anything simple about you. Including your—" she paused but hopefully managed to recover before he noticed "—wants."

"True," he agreed. "I do like things that

are…complicated. Hard to figure out. Makes the moment when you realize how to get what you want that much more rewarding." He grinned, the smile of a big bad wolf luring girls in red cloaks off the forest path. Despite the bright sunshine and summer temperature, Marguerite's skin prickled with awareness as if they were back in the dark, cool kitchen of the night before and his muscled thigh was warm beneath her leg.

"Have you ever failed?" she asked.

He shook his head slowly.

Of course it was a rhetorical question. She placed her elbows on the desk and leaned her chin onto her interlaced fingers, the better to keep her gaze steady. There's always a first time, you know."

"There's always the first time you approach a new situation. But you experiment. You learn. Take this, for example." He picked up a rose-colored foam ball from the desktop.

"Linus used that for stress relief. Do you need instructions?"

He turned the full force of his wolfish grin on her, and the ember of excitement, burning since the night before, kindled into a deep glow. "I'm familiar with stress relief. Although this? Not my preferred method."

Her throat was dry. She swallowed, hard. "I'm sure. Please, go ahead. You were saying?"

"It's a matter of action and reaction. For example, if I press here—" and his thumb made an indentation on the ball "—then I learn how soft it is. How pliant. And if I move like so..." His thumb made small circles on the surface of the ball. She couldn't tear her gaze away if she tried. Underneath the desk she crossed and uncrossed her legs, hoping that the movement would relieve the tension beginning to pool between them. It did not. "...now I know how the ball reacts to my touch."

She leaned back in her chair, hoping to affect an attitude as cool as the rest of her was hot. She wanted this job. She needed this job.

And mixing flirtation with business— much less going beyond flirtation—was a recipe for disaster. "Seems to me that ball is just lying there. Not quite sure I'd call that a reaction. Unless that's what you're used to. If so, no wonder you think you've never failed." She smiled, saccharine sweet.

His gaze flared with surprise and he laughed, placing the ball back on the desk. "As I said, I learn from whatever situation I'm in. Like what I've learned about you."

"Me? What could you have possibly learned about me in—" she checked her watch "—less than ten hours?"

"You don't take enough credit or compensation for your work. You're patient, or you wouldn't be in an industry that requires its product to age. You're a planner and don't follow your impulses—except maybe when your wine is involved, and then you had a plan for breaking in and taking it." His grin reappeared, big and bad and full of wicked promise. "How did I do?"

Better than she'd expected. She thought tech guys cared about only code: cold, lifeless numbers that flashed by on a bright screen in a dim, lonely room. But he'd laid her bare, one personality trait at a time. "That's not learning." She pretended to yawn. "That's amateur pop psychology."

He leaned over the desk. Only a few inches separated their mouths. He fixed her with his hazel gaze, a mesmerizing tumble of jade green, amber and russet. "And you don't like it when people get too close."

"Excuse me?" He wasn't wrong, but he also wasn't right. She did like having close relationships. The problem was when other people knew how much she cared, they used that knowledge to manipulate her. Betray her, even.

"Like now. You don't like it that I've picked up so much about you."

"Really."

He nodded. "Your lips," he rumbled, the vibrations putting the tiny hairs on her arms on alert.

"My lips?" She used her tongue to trace them.

His gaze followed the same path. "You purse your lips. When you're annoyed."

Her lips were indeed pursed. But it was also the shape of a mouth anticipating a kiss. And the light in his gaze told her he knew it, too.

She leaned back in her chair, seeking to get some distance from his delectable scent. This morning he was a cross between freshly laundered cotton, a hint of the lemongrass and basil from the night before, and a touch of black pepper and cardamom. For the first time in her life, she regretted having a finely attuned sense of smell. "That just means you can pick up on other people's tells. You must be one hell of a poker player."

He laughed. "True. My friends won't play with me."

"But I could be annoyed for a variety of reasons. For example, this is an annoying conversation."

"Annoying because I'm right." His grin was self-satisfied.

Their gazes battled. His was amused and... not unappreciative. He clearly enjoyed sparring with her. Learning how to get a reaction out of her.

She'd walked right into his trap. And unfortunately, she didn't mind at all. She could make herself very much at home, sharpening her wit to better play with him, watching the colors in his eyes shift and change as he responded.

But she also knew from experience how fast relationships could change, and one day she'd wake up and find herself shut out and left shivering, miserable and bereft. Casper had been her mentor and Linus a substitute grandfather, but while her caring for them had been platonic, when they left her, each in their own way, it had still been devastating.

Her initial reaction to Evan was anything but platonic. That spelled more potential trouble, and the situation had an even greater capacity to hurt her. The only way to deal with the heated charge hanging in the air between them was to spell out the rules of engagement from the start. She rose from her chair.

"Where are you going?"

"You don't already know? Since you know me so well." She pulled off the elastic band holding her messy bun in place, and her hair tumbled down. She then raised her arms to gather her hair back behind her neck, knowing the movement would display her chest to its best advantage. Sure enough, that caught his attention. She then walked around the desk and, facing him, hopped up on the surface, kicking off her sandals before crossing one leg over the other. The foot on top came perilously close to brushing his thighs when she swung it. "I'm being impulsive. Although—" she ran her gaze over his impressive physique, allowing it to linger on the areas that most interested her "—not as impulsive as I want to be."

"Oh?" His voice was a deep rumble. "What's stopping you?"

She shrugged. "Well, for one, it would involve the other party giving their consent."

"Let's say the other party does. Then what?"

"But it's more complicated than that, isn't it?" She tapped the manila folder containing the employment agreement. "I don't kiss coworkers. Or do anything else with coworkers, for that matter."

Recognition dawned in his expression, followed by a burst of horror. He ran a hand through his hair. "I don't, either. This is... not my usual behavior. I know better. I apologize. If you are having second thoughts about working for St. Isadore—"

"I'm working for St. Isadore." That was nonnegotiable. "It was my idea, remember? But—" she let her foot swing even closer to the top of his thigh "—I think we're both enjoying this...would you call it a flirtation?"

He didn't say anything, but the heat in his gaze gave her his response.

"So. Once I sign this document, I'm your employee. But until then—"

"—you're not." His slow smile made the breath catch in her throat.

"I'm not." She used her foot to spin his chair, so he faced away from her.

He leaned his head back so his upturned gaze could catch hers. "That wasn't what I was expecting."

She hopped off the desk. "Told you. I'm being impulsive."

Then she held his head steady with her hands. And lowered her mouth to his.

Embers exploded into fire. No wonder the upside-down kiss scene in the first Spider-Man movie was iconic. It turned the known geography of mouths into virgin territory, ripe for exploring.

He made a sound, or she did, she wasn't sure. He disengaged his mouth from hers, shrugging free from her light grip. But before she could register the loss of his heat against her, he was on his feet, tugging her to him, his grasp firm as he held her hips tight against him so she felt the solid shape of his arousal. Then it was his turn for his mouth to crash down on hers, demanding, insistent.

She'd been kissed before. By expert kissers who knew what they were doing and never gave her cause to complain. But Evan... Evan was in another class altogether. If kissing were an Olympic sport, they ultimately would have to force him to retire because no one could ever be better than him. And he was right. He did learn. Fast. He read her gasps and her sighs and knew exactly how to make her nerves sing.

She pulled away before her rational mind was taken over by pure want, while she could still control her hands and stop them from unbuttoning his shirt and roaming over his wide chest to explore the muscled skin that had haunted what little sleep she'd had the night before.

"Still think I can't act on impulse?" she said, struggling to return her breathing to something resembling normal.

He broke into a breathless chuckle. "Did I prove to you how much of a quick learner I am?"

"Your point is made." Her veins would not stop fizzing.

"So, if neither of us gets involved with colleagues…"

"Right." She walked back to her chair, hoping he couldn't tell how much her legs quivered, how her knees felt as if they would give way at any moment. "That was fun. But we also agree we don't kiss—or engage in any other physical activity—with coworkers." She pulled the employment contract toward her. He watched her through hooded eyes as she flipped to the last page, took out her pen and let it hover about the line for her signature. "Once I sign this, our relationship is strictly professional. Agreed?"

A light flared in his eyes but was quickly extinguished. "Two consenting adults had a good time, but now comes the hard work. I won't lie. I do find you attractive. But I also promise you can trust me. My self-control is rock-solid."

That isn't the only thing about you that's rock-solid... She shook her head. They had a moment, they sated their curiosity, and now they could work without constant static disrupting the atmosphere. Her libido would stay locked up in solitary confinement for the duration of her employment contract. She would not be thrown off track from her goal of restoring the Delacroix name to wine-making prominence.

But she also wouldn't lie. She found Evan damn attractive.

"I look forward to a productive working relationship." She scrawled her name and dated the document before handing it to him. "Let's start."

Four

Evan leaned back in his desk chair and stared out the window of his San Francisco office, high in a tower that afforded him a prime view of the bay. It was a clear, bright summer day, absent the fog for which the city was famous. Sailboats blew this way and that over the water's surface as ferry boats took tourists to and from Alcatraz Island, but he didn't see them. Instead, his mind fixated on the distant Golden Gate Bridge and the rolling hills on the opposite side. It was Friday afternoon. If he left now and took the bridge, he would be in Napa in ninety minutes and have the whole weekend there…

"The meeting with the suppliers is Tuesday. We need to nail them down before we speak to the bank next week and—" Luke Dallas put down his electronic tablet and looked up from where he sat in the guest chair opposite Evan's desk. "Evan? You with me?"

"Huh?" Evan dragged his gaze away from the window and the route that would take him to St. Isadore. Although technically Luke was the chief operating officer and Evan was the chief executive officer of Medevco Technologies, they ran the business as a team. A smoothly operating team, so Evan didn't know why Luke sounded so testy. "Sure. I'm with you. The meeting is Thursday."

"Tuesday," Luke corrected. He leaned forward. "Anything you need to tell me?"

"No. Why? The distribution situation is finally in hand. Three weeks of round-the-clock worry I'm never going to get back, but otherwise, a return to optimal. But it underlines why we need to nail down that investment from Angus Horne." Evan glanced out the window again. A flash of sunlight off the water caught his gaze. He followed the trail of light to the bridge again. Traffic would be dense, but it would be worse if he left an hour from now. If he wrapped things up—

"So you keep saying." Luke didn't sound happy, but Luke usually sounded terse. The only times Evan heard him laugh was when Luke was with his wife, Danica.

"You don't need me for anything for the rest of the day, right? I'd like to head out to the winery." Evan began to organize his desktop, straightening papers and putting away unneeded items.

Luke's gaze narrowed. "The company needs us to figure out this supply chain problem. Or we won't have a company."

Evan closed his top drawer and locked it. "Alarming. Also, not true."

"But now I have your attention." Luke tapped on the surface of his tablet. "I sent you the information for the supplier meeting on *Tuesday*—" he stressed the last word "—so don't extend your stay in Napa past Monday. No matter how attractive she is."

"Don't worry. I'll be ready—" He froze, his laptop half in, half out of the carrying bag. "What makes you think there's a she?"

Luke never rolled his eyes. But his expression was the closest thing Evan had seen to an eye roll in their year or so of partnership. "You're moody and easily distracted. There's no other logical explanation."

"There are plenty of explanations. Nico, for example. Nico is more than enough of an explanation."

"Right. Nico. The brother I didn't know you had until you brought him to the office last month. Yes, you've always been concerned about spending as much time as you can with him."

Ouch.

Evan liked Luke. A lot. He was the best business partner Evan had ever had in two decades of creating start-ups and building them into success stories acquired by larger companies for hefty sums of money. He'd envisioned being partners with Luke for a long time. Until now. "Just because I don't turn into goop when my family is mentioned—"

"Goop? What are you—?"

"Danica," Evan shot back at him.

A warm smile replaced Luke's taciturn expression.

"See?" Evan said. "Goop. As soon as you hear her name."

"I wasn't aware *goop* was the technical term for caring about one's wife." Luke rose from his chair and crossed the room to leave. "Enjoy the weekend. But don't forget about Tuesday."

"I won't." Evan waved Luke off and went back to packing his work bag in preparation for the trip ahead.

He wasn't leaving now to see Marguerite. He did need to spend time with Nico. Nico, whose resentment of him must be ready to erupt like a geyser for dragging him to Napa and dumping him in an ancient mansion while Evan went back to San Francisco to work. Nico, who—

Images of tousled waves of dark hair piled into a messy bun crowded everything else out of his brain. Dark brown eyes, so dark he almost missed the dilation of her pupils after she kissed him. Pale skin that, no matter how nonchalant and unaffected she pretended to be, betrayed with a flush her true emotions.

He'd spoken on the phone with Marguerite every day during the last three weeks. Her conversation revealed her bright wit, delivered through dry asides and wry jokes that kept him laughing. He found her intriguing—after all, she'd broken into his house and he'd ended up hiring her—and he wouldn't be averse to kissing her again and letting things build to their inevitable conclusion, preferably in a nearby bed. But that's where any entanglement with her stopped.

There would be no goop—aka mooning after a hypothetical wife—in his future. He would not walk around the office with a goofy smile on his face like Luke did after receiving a text from Danica. Not now, and not in the future.

Relationships took time, energy and resources. He was only human and he had limited supply of each. He knew his strengths and where he could maximize his returns. If he had returned home after his parents died and taken custody of five-year-old Nico as his grandparents had suggested, he wouldn't have been able to develop his ideas, work on the code, hire additional developers, network with investors, meet with buyers. And he wouldn't possess the money now to ensure Nico didn't need to struggle the way Evan had. To set Nico up in a career he loved, to pave the way so his journey would be far smoother than Evan's.

He'd done the right thing then, and he was doing the right thing now. Nico had had a good childhood with their grandparents, and now that he was a young man, Evan would help him find his way. Therefore, he was eager to get to St. Isadore for one reason only: to ensure his investment was in good hands as long as it took for either Nico to take over or for Evan to sell it at a profit and reinvest the money in another occupation for his brother.

Besides, Marguerite was his employee. They had a contract. They'd both made it clear they did not indulge in personal relationships at work.

By the time he crossed the Golden Gate Bridge, visions of tumbled black curls and darkly slumberous eyes, dazed with passion, filled his head.

Marguerite stared at her computer screen. Her entire day had been spent answering questions. Her in-box should be nearly empty. But as she scrolled, the number of unread emails continued to climb. She picked one at random, read the first line and clicked away almost immediately, screwing her eyes shut.

With Evan called back to San Francisco for an emergency at his tech company, the responsibility for St. Isadore's day-to-day operations fell on her shoulders. Although they talked every day, what Evan knew about the industry would fit on a wine label and still leave room for the logo and the government warning about sulfites. She had assisted Linus, but she hadn't realized until now how much work Linus kept to himself. No wonder the winery had suffered as Linus's health declined.

There was so much that needed to be accomplished. Aside from ramping up the winemaking operations, the tasting room needed to be remodeled and brought into the twenty-first century. The main building required a laundry list of repairs. And their distribution network was on life support and must be rebuilt, along with their sales team.

They were close to hiring a director of operations, and she had a stack of resumes to give to Evan for the other open jobs. Once St. Isadore was fully staffed, things would run more smoothly, but what made Marguerite think she could get the business to that stage? And what had possessed her to tell Evan she could?

Her own damn pride, that's what. And loyalty. Family honor. At least as long as she was at St. Isadore, she could continue her quest to return the Delacroix name to its legendary winemaking status.

Assuming she kept her job through the next few weeks, much less the next six months.

She groaned and folded her arms on her desk, the better to pillow her forehead while she tried to decide which urgent priority to tackle next.

"I have broken down the event for the Global Leader Summit into steps." Aracely breezed into the office, looking like she was ready to take her seat in the front row at Paris Fashion Week instead of an office in Napa. Her dark olive complexion was flawlessly made up, her ebony hair piled on top of her head in a complicated twist. She stopped short and her long skirt billowed around her legs. "You haven't spent the entire day napping, I hope?"

Marguerite raised her head. "Steps? You have next steps?" Something like hope blossomed inside her.

"Of course. That is why you recommended me to be the event planner." Aracely put a binder stuffed with pages on Marguerite's desk and took the chair opposite her. A vision of Evan in that chair flashed across Marguerite's mind. How his mouth had opened under hers, his tongue sweeping hers, his hands—

"That is also why you're paying me the big money." Aracely wagged her eyebrows, earning a laugh from Marguerite.

"Why Evan is paying you," she corrected.

"Right, Evan. I am still impressed you turned a break-in into a job offer. Not to mention a place to live."

"The carriage house was empty and could use a paying tenant." Marguerite shrugged. "I know, because I was the last person to live in it. It was a no-brainer."

Aracely smirked as she tapped the binder. "This contains sketches for the party layout, photos of possible decorations and some fabric samples for the tablecloths as well as the shirts for the serving staff. Oh, and speaking of clothes, I dropped off a few things for you at your place. Some pieces of mine you might want to borrow for the party. Or any other occasion now that you're back at St. Isadore."

"That wasn't necessary," Marguerite answered automatically, but she gave Aracely a wide smile. Aracely's wardrobe truly was a wonder to behold. Not only did she possess exquisite taste and the funds to indulge it but she'd also inherited closets of designer clothes from her mother and grandmother, both noted socialites in their youth.

"Just a few things." Aracely pushed the binder toward her. "Here. Look."

Marguerite flipped through the pages. On top were drawings of the winery's terrace with various configurations of furniture and food stations. Underneath a divider were mood boards containing color palettes, suggested lighting configurations and flower arrangements for the tables. And below another divider, she found cloth samples and examples of various embroidery styles so the servers' uniforms would proudly proclaim they worked for St. Isadore. "All I see are decisions that need to be made." She pushed the binder back at Aracely. "My head is spinning. You do it."

"Pobrecita." Aracely didn't sound sympathetic. "If you want to run a winery, hosting events will be an important part of your revenue stream. Start with the first page and go one by one."

Marguerite sighed. Aracely was right. Becoming a sought-after venue for meetings and celebrations was vital to the stability of St. Isadore's financial health. "Sorry. Momentary moment of mortification. Won't happen again."

"Yes, it will. You are human." Aracely grinned. "But this is exciting! We get to spend someone else's money. My favorite form of exercise."

"You do like to give credit cards a workout." Marguerite opened the binder to the beginning section, removing the pages so she could arrange them on her desk. "Start with the layout first, then decorations?"

"Then the details." Aracely nodded. "I will be cheeky and tell you my favorites."

"In case I choose wrong."

"But of course," Aracely agreed with an angelic smile. "My reputation is riding on this as much as yours."

Marguerite looked up from the first sketch. "What are you talking about? You've only been in Napa three years, and you're one of the most sought-after event planners around. Besides, you're going back to Chile in December. Which I'm not forgiving you for, by the way. I don't care how much your parents' business needs you."

"The business does not need me." The smile stayed on Aracely's face, but it no longer reached her eyes. "My parents want me to return."

"But to take over the business, right?"

Aracely made an impatient gesture. "It does not matter why. Now, do you prefer to set up the area for dining on the north end of the terrace or the south end? Here are several different layouts."

"If you don't want to go back, you should tell them."

Aracely kept her gaze focused on the sketches. "I think the north end. It is more protected from the wind."

"You know I'm here if you need to discuss anything."

A flash lit Aracely's gaze, so quickly Marguerite didn't know if she saw it or imagined it. "I will figure it out, like I am figuring out the wine tasting without your help. Care to join in? I am assuming Evan will want to know the plans." Her familiar smirk appeared on her lips. "Or not. Perhaps this is only pretend so he can canoodle more with you."

"Canoodle? What old movie did you learn that from?"

"Aha! This suggests I used the right word as you are not disputing the meaning."

Marguerite rolled her eyes. "There's no canoodling. Not now, not in the future. Especially not with people I work with."

Aracely shook her head. "And yet you and Evan canoodled."

"Can we stop using that word? There's nothing going on. I kissed him to prove a point, nothing more. Now he's my employer, and that's the end of the relationship between us." Marguerite stabbed at the first piece of paper she saw on her desk. "Here. Let's go with this one."

Aracely picked it up. "This is a letter from the sanitation department about the proper disposal of refuse. It will be a stretch to make this work for the wine tasting, but I have an excellent imagination."

Marguerite snatched the letter back. "Set up the food tables on the north end. Because of the wind."

"Excellent choice. So, chairs. Do you want—?"

Marguerite's cell phone rang, cutting off Aracely midsentence. Marguerite looked at the caller ID. "It's Nico."

Although Nico had stayed at St. Isadore after Evan returned to San Francisco, she rarely saw him and they exchanged even fewer words. Why would he call her? Her mind raced to several conclusions, and she didn't like any of them. "Hello?"

Nico didn't bother with a greeting. "Evan's not with you, is he?"

"Um, no." Why would Nico think that? What did Evan say—?

"I was hoping he was back from San Francisco." Nico's voice was strained as if he were in pain.

"Sorry, I haven't seen him. Are you okay?"

He was silent for a few beats. "There was a…thing. I need a ride."

"Are you hurt? Do you need to go to the hospital?"

"I'm fine. My friend, too. We just need to get out of here. We tried to order a rideshare, but no cars are available."

"Are you safe?"

He huffed into the phone as if catching his breath. "Yeah. Now."

"Do you know where you are? Give me the address." She wrote it down. "I'll be right there." She got up from her desk, grabbed her purse and car keys. "If by any chance you see or hear from Evan, let him know I'm on my way to get Nico," she called to Aracely as she exited.

Nico was in a community over forty-five minutes away, which wasn't so much of a town as a collection of gas stations, food markets, and the odd restaurant and wine-tasting room. Luckily, the traffic was light on the back roads skirting the various vineyards, and she was able to get to him in record time.

He paced outside a convenience store, his hands thrust in his jeans pockets, his thin shoulders hunched around his ears. She pulled into the parking space in front of him. "I'm here," she called out the window.

Nico's shoulders fell, but he retained his air of guarded wariness. "One minute," he said, and he disappeared into the store. When he emerged, he was escorting a young woman. He didn't touch her, but it was evident from the way he bent his head to listen to her and curved his body as if to shield her that she must be the friend he'd mentioned on the phone.

Or more than a friend.

Nico opened the rear passenger door and escorted the woman inside the car and then came around to the other rear door and slid in behind the driver's seat. "Thanks for picking us up," he said. "This is Gabi. Gabi, this is Marguerite."

Gabi raised her head and caught Marguerite's gaze in the rearview mirror. "Thanks for taking time out of your day. We appreciate it. I called my friends but they're all at work and couldn't leave."

Marguerite could see why Nico liked Gabi. She was a pretty brunette with dark brown skin, a direct gaze and straightforward manner. Marguerite nodded. "No problem. So, what happened?"

Nico peered out his window. "Do you mind if we start moving first?"

"Sure." Marguerite reversed out of the parking space and put the car in Drive. When they reached the main road, she threw a glance via the mirror at the couple in the rear seat. "This is all very cloak-and-dagger-ish. Want to tell me what happened now?"

Gabi leaned forward. "I'm an intern at Dellavina Cellars. In winemaking."

Something slithery crawled in Marguerite's stomach. "You work for Casper Vos."

"Right. Anyway, we all went out for drinks the other day—all the interns, that is. And Nico was at the same place and we…"

"Started talking," Nico supplied.

"Yes. And we both had to leave, but we've stayed in touch. So when I had today off, I suggested Nico and I meet up this afternoon to go for a bike ride, explore some more of Napa." Gabi sighed.

The uneasiness in Marguerite's stomach expanded, although at least it was no longer connected to Casper. "I didn't see bikes when I picked you up."

Gabi shook her head. "No."

Marguerite glanced at the couple via the rearview mirror again. "Were they stolen?"

"I got a flat. We pulled off the road to patch the tire." Nico's voice was a good impersonation of a volcano struggling not to blow and let loose lava flows of hot anger. "Then these guys drove by, yelling trash at Gabi. We didn't think anything of it. Fifteen minutes later, they came back from the other direction."

"How awful." Marguerite kept her focus on the road, but her heart was with the couple in the back seat. "I'm so sorry."

"They probably had too much to drink. But when they drove by the third time, we decided to ditch the bikes and hike across some fields to the nearest safe place," Gabi said. "And that's when we called you."

"I'm glad I answered. Do you want me to send a truck out to collect the bikes?"

"If they're still there." In the rearview mirror, Nico's lips pressed together in a thin, hard line. "They belong to Dellavina, so we should try to return them."

Marguerite nodded. "I'm going to call the sheriff. Do you have a description of their car?" Then she realized she was almost at the turnoff for the long driveway that led to St. Isadore. "I'm so sorry, I'm driving on autopilot. Gabi, where should I take you?"

"Gabi's staying with me." Nico's tone was ironclad. "And I memorized the license plate number."

Marguerite bypassed the turnoff for the winery and kept going. "Why don't you both come to my place? It's more comfortable than the winery office, and we can call the sheriff together."

Every San Franciscan in possession of a car had decided to visit Napa for the weekend, or so it seemed to Evan after it took three hours—spent on phone calls trying to schedule a meeting with Angus Horne's people—to reach St. Isadore. He couldn't wait to get out of the car, pour himself a glass of one of Marguerite's wines and spend some time catching up on what had happened at the winery in his absence.

It was only eight o'clock. Marguerite tended to work late. Perhaps she wouldn't mind coming up to the house, with its dark corners and overstuffed furniture creating an intimate atmosphere no matter the size of the rooms. A vision of her sitting next to him, a circle of warm light encompassing both of them as they discussed her plans, danced in his head.

For once, he didn't mind the Gothic haunted house aesthetic.

But when he entered the owner's residence, there was a stillness to the rooms that indicated no one was home. And when he pulled back the curtains to check on the winery offices across the large flagstone terrace, Marguerite's window was dark. Nico, sure. He didn't expect a young adult male to hang around an empty house waiting for an older brother when there were bars and clubs and other people his age not too far away. Marguerite, on the other hand... Her absence delivered a right hook that he hadn't seen coming.

He rolled his eyes at himself. Of course she had better things to do on a Friday night than sit at her desk, waiting for her boss to arrive so she could debrief him. But he'd thought... maybe...she'd want to see him since it had been three weeks since they were last in a room together.

He looked at his phone. There were several missed calls from Nico. Well, at the least, the kid was keeping him informed of his comings and goings after that first night. Evan pressed the callback button as he searched the meager offerings in the refrigerator. Looked like Nico hadn't grocery shopped, either. Again, not that he blamed him.

"Hey," Nico answered. There was laughter and even music in the background, but it didn't sound like he was at a club. Someone's house?

"Hey," Evan replied. "I'm home. Where are you?"

"Marguerite's place." Someone said something to Nico Evan couldn't quite hear. "Got to go. See you later." He hung up.

Evan stared at the phone in his hand. Nico was at Marguerite's apartment? At eight o'clock on a Friday night?

What the hell was going on? And why was there music?

Not that he was jealous of his baby brother. But were they having a party? Without him? They both knew he was returning tonight.

This was why he'd made the right decision all those years ago. He should be spending his Friday night out with business associates, wining and dining, building his networks of contacts, working ever closer to his goal of creating a multinational empire. Medevco was the closest he had come so far to starting something that might actually still be a major corporate player in people's lives twenty years from now. And while much of its product success was due to Luke and his technical genius, Evan had brought in the investors who provided the money to keep the company growing. He'd partnered with Grayson Monk and his venture capital firm. He charmed the banks. He made the rounds of Wall Street firms. He was going to bring Angus Horne on board for their biggest round of financing yet, thus solving several of their growing pains.

That's what he was good at. That's how he provided value for the people in his life.

Evan grabbed a beer out of the refrigerator, slammed the door shut and headed for the back door and the mile walk to the carriage house. He could drive, but the thought of being behind the wheel again so soon made his spine ache. Besides, he could use the exercise. And the cool night air.

By the time his destination was in sight, he had worked up a sweat and finished the beer, which provided him with a thin layer of calm. Until he got close enough and saw a sheriff's car pull away from the converted stables that held garages for various winery vehicles, with Marguerite's apartment above.

He broke into a run, somehow not tripping on the cobblestones that made up the courtyard entrance. The ground floor front door was unlocked, and he took the stairs two at a time to the residential quarters on the second floor, bursting into Marguerite's living room and almost falling on his face at his abrupt stop. He windmilled his arms to keep his balance.

Three heads swiveled as if one to gape at him.

"Why was? The sheriff here?" he gasped between gulps of needed oxygen. "Again?" His vision recovered enough to take in the sight before him. Marguerite was standing in the middle of the room, her arms akimbo as if striking a pose. A young Black woman about Nico's age sat on the sofa. Nico lounged in an armchair opposite, while the empty chair next to him held what looked like a pile of dresses. The low coffee table held three wineglasses and a mostly empty wine bottle as well as bowls of popcorn and potato chips. Music softly played in the background.

He had interrupted some sort of gathering.

Marguerite recovered her aplomb first and lowered her arms. "Hello, Evan. Welcome to my home. As for your questions, the sheriff was in the neighborhood and stopped by to take Nico's and Gabi's statements," she said as if that explained everything. She frowned and plucked the empty beer can from his nerveless grasp, holding it up. "Seriously?"

"What? Why? Who?" His lungs still felt as though a brush fire had been kindled inside them.

"Nico and Gabi." Marguerite indicated the young woman next to her. "Evan, this is Gabi Watkins, Nico's friend. She's a college intern at Dellavina Cellars. Gabi, this is Nico's brother, Evan. The new owner of St. Isadore." Gabi waved hello as Marguerite continued, "They were out for a bike ride this afternoon, and men in a car harassed them. The sheriff has a description and license plate number and said he would keep an eye out."

"Wait. Slow down." He got his breathing under control. "One thing at a time. Bike ride?" He turned to Nico. "You were supposed to shadow the accountants while I was in the city."

Nico's lower lip jutted out. "That's what you took away from what Marguerite said? I didn't do as you told me?"

"I said one thing at a time. That was the first thing." Evan ran a hand through his hair. Why was it so hard to hold a simple conversation with his brother? He never had this problem talking to his staff.

"Maybe 'Are you okay?' should be the first thing. Or 'Sorry that happened to you.'" The darkness clouding Nico's expression was turning into a full-blown storm. "No, the first thing should have been 'Hi, Gabi, nice to meet you.'" He got out of his chair and extended his right hand to Gabi. "Come on, let's go."

"Nico—" Evan sputtered.

"Nico." Marguerite's soft tone seemed to cause Nico to visibly relax. "Evan just got here. Give him some time to catch up. Gabi, why don't you see if a friend is available to pick you up?" She pointed at Evan. "You. Come with me, please."

"You know I'm the boss, right?" Evan grumbled, but he followed her.

Marguerite led him to a small balcony off the dining room. After sliding the glass door shut behind them, she turned to him with a magnificent scowl on her face. "Of course, I know you're the boss. Until now. I quit."

"Good. So, as the boss—" His ears caught up with her words. "Wait. You what?"

* * *

"You'll probably fire me anyway. I'm just saving you the trouble." Marguerite took a deep breath, willing her voice not to tremble. She was taking a huge risk. He might indeed demand she leave St. Isadore. But she had spent the last two hours getting to know Nico better and he deserved a champion. Which meant inserting herself into the brothers' private lives. "We agreed that after we signed the agreement our relationship would be professional only. But this is about your personal life."

He narrowed his gaze. "I doubt I'd fire you for voicing your opinion, personal or not. Go for it."

"You must stop treating Nico like a child. Or like someone you pay." She folded her arms across her chest, the better to hide her still quaking fingers, and gave him her best glare. "You're his brother, not his boss."

She expected his anger to flare or perhaps his disdain. Instead, his eyebrows rose as his gaze swept over her. "I'm familiar with casual Friday, but this is the first I've heard of formal Friday. St. Isadore tradition?"

What was he—? "If this is an attempt to deflect the conservation away from you and Nico—"

He waved a hand at her outfit. "You look great, by the way."

She glanced down and her cheeks filled with heat. "Right. Sorry. I was trying to take Nico's and Gabi's minds off what happened. Aracely dropped off some dresses for me to try on for the event, so we were playing fashion show." She smoothed her hands over the full skirt of the 1950s-era emerald green cocktail dress she wore. "You should see Gabi in this Pucci minidress that used to belong to Aracely's grandmother."

He ran his gaze over her one more time, slow and deliberate. "I like what I'm seeing now. Since we're being personal."

Her cheeks were hot enough to start a brushfire. "We're talking about you, not me."

He cleared this throat. "Go ahead. You called me out here to yell at me."

"Not yell. I just don't understand why you and Nico constantly go from zero to being at each other's throats in five-point-six seconds." She tried to search his gaze, but he evaded her attempts.

"I wasn't at his throat. I asked him a reasonable question." He leaned against the sliding glass door. The lamp glow from inside threw his muscled physique into silhouette.

"They were scared today. Badly. You didn't even ask how they were."

"You all seemed perfectly relaxed when I came in."

"After I distracted them and got their minds off what happened! You need to pay more attention to him."

He straightened up. "I do pay attention. Why do you think he's here? Why do you think I bought St. Isadore?"

"Honestly? I have no idea."

"It's for him. He flunked out of college and needs an occupation. That's why we're here. For Nico to learn a business. Get his hands dirty. You say I'm not his employer. But I am."

"Wait. You bought St. Isadore for Nico? As a...toy?" Her voice rose on the last word. All of her hard work. Her family's history. But to Evan, St. Isadore was nothing but a play-thing?

"No, not as a toy—"

"You run a tech company. Why not find a job for him there? You think you can throw anyone into running St. Isadore?"

"I threw *you* into running St. Isadore."

She scoffed. "That's different."

"How?"

"Because I..." She stopped, worrying her lower lip with her teeth. Earlier, she'd wondered if she was the right person to oversee St. Isadore. But she'd raised her hand for the job. Evan barely acknowledged Nico's presence. She doubted if he had even asked Nico if this was what he wanted. She tilted her chin high and met his gaze. "Because I know what it entails. I have experience."

"Exactly. And so will Nico if he would wake up." He made a sweeping motion with his hand, indicating the bulky shadow of the winery in the near distance. "How many kids his age are given such an opportunity? He's squandering it."

"He took one afternoon off to spend time with a woman he likes."

"And then one afternoon turns into a week. Then a month. Before Nico knows it, the year will go by and he'll have nothing to show for it."

"He might have a relationship to show for it."

Evan laughed, a deep belly guffaw. "Right. That's supposed to make up for wasting the chance to learn how to run a company from the ground up. What's he going to do when she goes back to school? You said she was an intern, right?"

"Yes, but you're missing the point—"

"She'll go back to her classes and friends. Nico will be nothing but a brief memory. And he'll have no education. No school no school of hard knocks."

"You don't know that—"

"You think I need to pay attention to Nico? I am paying. Attention and money. Lots of money. This place sucks up resources like a tornado. But I'm willing to throw cash at it so Nico has a future. A future that wouldn't be his if I didn't care so much." He gave Marguerite a firm nod.

She regarded him for a beat. "Can I speak now?"

"What more needs to be said?"

"Do you genuinely think Nico should be, what was it, stuck inside all day with accountants—?"

"Shadowing accountants. So he can learn. Man, I wish I had done that when I started out. If you can't read a spreadsheet or understand a financial report, you are—"

She cleared her throat, cutting him off. "I thought there was nothing left to be said."

He held both his hands up in a gesture of apology. "Sorry. You were saying."

"Is this what you did when you were Nico's age? Spent your time indoors pouring over numbers instead of going out? Falling in love?"

He grinned. "I fell many times. Several times a night. I'm all for Nico enjoying himself as much as he wants."

Good thing she gave him her verbal notice and could consider herself officially unemployed. This was definitely not terrain she should be exploring with her boss. No matter how interested she was in his side of the conversation. "I'm not talking about sex. I'm talking about love."

"There's not a lot of difference between the two at the age of twenty-one."

"Of course there is! Nico and Gabi are exhibit A."

Evan scoffed. "This is the first I've heard Gabi's name. Sure, Nico might be infatuated. She's very attractive. But love? They just met. He's too young to know if it's love."

Marguerite stopped herself from rolling her eyes. "And what is the age for knowing your own heart, O wise one? Twenty-five? Thirty-two? Fifty-seven?"

"You know I'm right. You don't want to admit it."

"Have you ever been in love?" This time she caught his gaze. His eyes were dark and unreadable in the dim light. The longer their gazes held, the faster her pulse sped up. He wouldn't break the connection, and she couldn't.

He looked away first, to her satisfaction. Or her disappointment. It was hard to tell with her heart threatening to jump out of her chest. "Hasn't everyone? After one breakup, I even grew a beard and bought out an entire liquor store of its whiskey."

"I'm sorry. That sounds like it was painful."

"Then I shaved and threw a party. My friends drank what was left in the liquor cabinet, and that was that." He shifted his position to lean on the railing next to her. "What about you? When were you old enough to know if you were in love or only in love with the, let's say, physical feeling?"

The night breeze carried his scent to her. Still the hint of basil and lemongrass but with a deeper, richer base note she was coming to think of as "Evan." She inhaled deeply before she knew what she was doing. "I think… you're born knowing. But it takes the right person to switch it on, no matter how old you are."

"And have you been switched on?" he rumbled.

The night breeze had subsided, leaving the world still and hushed. Stars glowed high overhead in a moonless, dark indigo sky, leaving the light spilling from the sliding glass door as the only source of illumination. She was keenly aware that Evan was less than an arm's length away, so close she could reach out and hold his hand.

Draw him to her.

She shook her head to clear it. "I'm not the subject here. Look, I don't know the history between you and Nico. And maybe it's the age difference that makes you two butt heads every time I see you together. But even as his employer, you can't stick him in an office and walk away and not expect him to be resentful. You especially can't fault him for spending time with Gabi. He has genuine feelings for her."

The moment—if there had even been one—dissipated. He leaned away from her. "I know where those feelings originate, and it's not his heart. It's another organ. That's fine, as long they both consent and take necessary health precautions. But spending time with her when he should be working isn't going to pay his bills. He needs to learn that. And he's damn lucky he has me to give him that opportunity."

The wind blew Marguerite's hair into her face, and she pushed it back with an impatient movement. "Okay. Fine. You're his brother."

"Yes, I am." He threw her a side-eyed glance. "But. You're not wrong. We do butt heads whenever we're together. Tonight is the most relaxed I've seen him since he came out to California."

"I spent the last two hours talking with him and Gabi." She reached over to touch Evan's hand but chickened out and drew back at the last second. "You should try it."

"I didn't mean to leave him here by himself for so long, but—" He shrugged. "Things at Medevco seem to be in constant crisis. We grew very fast. Now we need to secure another round of money so we can continue to expand, or we need to make cuts. And we're not making cuts." His tone was final. But she didn't miss the almost imperceptible flash of concern in his eyes. Perhaps he was capable of deeper caring, after all.

"Nico knows how important your company is to you. He does. But while he's here in Napa and you're there in San Francisco, have you thought about having him work in hospitality or retail instead of accounting? The gift shop, for example. He likes people and he's knowledgeable about wine. He'd need a refresher course on St. Isadore's offerings, but then he'd be ready to give people recommendations."

Evan shook his head. "I've got a better idea. Nico reports to you."

"Me? You forgot. I quit."

"Your contract requires a written letter of resignation with fourteen days of notice. Until I accept it, you're still employed." He smiled.

She laughed. "I guess we're back to being professional colleagues."

His little finger brushed hers. Accidentally, she was sure. Her heart skipped a beat nonetheless. "I like to think this conversation took place between friends," he said.

"Friends?" Her laughter faded. "I don't know. Work and relationships, even when it's friendship, don't mix well in my experience—"

He nodded. "Right. Our contract talk. I remember." The deep rumble of his voice, accompanied by the devilish glint in his gaze, told her exactly what he remembered. Her knees turned to water. Thankfully, her fingers were locked in a death grip on the balcony railing. "Outside work. During work, I need to pretend I know what I'm doing when it comes to St. Isadore. For the sake of my poor, deluded ego."

She laughed to buy herself time and give her legs a chance to recover their strength. "See, this is why I would never claim to be able to read you. You say things like that out of the blue."

"So, what do you say? Friends?"

She shouldn't say yes. Being friends with Casper had led to letting her guard down, only to be sucker-punched when he took credit for her ideas and used them to secure a more prestigious position, bad-mouthing her in the process. She thought Linus had cared for her as a family member instead of just a disposable employee, and it had nearly broken her when she discovered how wrong she had been.

But being friends with Evan had its appeal. Especially if it meant she could help him with his relationship with Nico. And she had to admit she liked spending time with Evan. She wouldn't mind getting to know him better.

To make her job easier, of course. No other reason. Or so she lied to herself.

She mimed raising a glass in a toast. "To friendship. After hours."

He held up his own imaginary glass, and in the process, their hands briefly tangled. Heat flared where his skin slid against hers.

She was pretty sure friends didn't feel a friend's touch hours later.

It was a long, sleepless night.

Five

Marguerite crossed another day off the wall calendar hanging behind her desk and leaned back in her chair. Nine weeks ago, she'd broken into St. Isadore. Six weeks ago, she and Evan had decided to be friends.

That left three months to go until the Global Leader Summit event.

Would she make it?

St. Isadore wasn't the cause of her concern, for once. After reviewing the business plan she drew up, she and Evan agreed the winery needed more staff. They'd recently finished the interview process and made a series of job offers, including a director of operations who would take some of the day-to-day responsibilities off Marguerite's shoulders. The winery would soon operate at full capacity again, and the upcoming harvest crush and fermentation no longer featured prominently in her nightmares. And despite being looked after by a near-skeletal operation after Linus's death, the wine aging in barrels was promising. The Cabernet Sauvignon still needed more time, but the Chardonnay was almost ready to be bottled. They wouldn't produce nearly as many cases as they should this year, but St. Isadore was in better shape than it had been for some time.

But before she could get to harvest in late summer, she had to get through the upcoming Global Leader Summit event.

Which meant spending more time with Evan, who'd called ninety minutes ago to say he was leaving San Francisco for St. Isadore.

Gone were the often stilted conversations of her first few weeks working with him. Since that evening on the balcony, their phone discussions ebbed and flowed naturally.

But talking long-distance only went so far. Although they occasionally used video when

Marguerite needed to run items past him for approval, for the most part Evan remained a disembodied presence in her ear. He usually called late at night after marathon hours at Medevco, and at first, his tone would be terse, even impatient. But after an exchange of pleasantries and comparison of their work schedules, he'd slow down, his voice deepening, his conversation turning thoughtful or roguish, with the occasional rumbling of laughter.

It was the best part of her day. Alone in her room, tucked in her bed, the lights out and only his voice tethering her to the world, it was so easy to pretend she and Evan were actual friends.

Or more.

Which was why she had yet to tell him about her agreement with Linus granting her ownership of the original Delacroix vineyard. Or even to confess that she was descended from St. Isadore's original owner. She didn't want to do or say anything that could damage the growing but fragile trust building between them. And she certainly didn't want to throw any wrenches into the relationship tentatively forming between him and Nico.

A knock sounded at her door, and as if her thoughts had summoned him, Nico appeared. He carried a large box in his hands. "Okay if I take off a little early? Gabi's parents are in town. They scored reservations at La Blanchisserie and asked me to join them."

"Wow. Those are difficult reservations to get. Parents, huh?" Marguerite couldn't help the large smile spreading across her face.

Nico ducked his head. "Not a big deal."

Marguerite rarely saw the family resemblance between Nico and his brother, but she heard it in their speech. Nico had the same don't-push-any-further warning tone in his voice as Evan whenever the subject got too close to his personal danger zone. She nodded at the box in his hands. "Is that the wine aroma kit?"

Nico put it down on her desk. "Thanks for letting me borrow it. Gabi and I have been practicing. I thought I had a decent nose, but hers? Wow."

"I bet yours is pretty good." Marguerite glanced at the clock. Evan could arrive at any minute. Or he might be stuck in traffic and not arrive for hours. She was too jumpy to sit at her desk and pretend to answer the emails that had come in while she was out in the vineyards. "Do you have time before you go to show off what you learned?"

Nico's eyes lit up. "I've got a half hour. What do you have in mind?"

"Want to help with my Chardonnay trials?"

"Sure. Are we going to the cellars?"

She shook her head. "I'll have samples brought up to us. I don't want to miss Evan." She fired off a message, catching a glimpse of her reflection in the computer monitor. She smoothed her hair, gathering up loose locks and tucking them back into her ponytail. She wouldn't be able to do anything about her wrinkled shirt. She brushed at it anyway.

Nico sat down in the guest chair. The chair she still couldn't look at without blushing. "Don't want to miss him, huh?"

She glanced around the monitor and caught his smirk. "He's my boss and he's been in San Francisco all week. I have some items to discuss with him."

"You could send him an email." Nico's grin grew, threatening to reach his ears.

Two could play that game. "So, Gabi's parents. First time meeting them?"

Nico wiped his expression clear, and he scratched the back of his neck. "I was thinking, if it's okay with you, my next rotation could be in the tasting room."

She hid her own smile. "Tired of winemaking already?"

He gave her a one-shouldered shrug. "There's a lot of chemistry involved. And math."

She nodded her head. "Indeed."

"I like talking about wine. And drinking it, of course. But maybe not making it. Not the way you and Gabi like making it. It's like a calling for you two. For me it's more of a... fun hobby."

She inhaled. "You know why Evan bought this place, right?"

A knock on her door heralded the arrival of the wine samples. She thanked the messenger and took the eight small, labeled glasses, placing them on her desk. Four for her, four for Nico. "Saved by the bell. Or the wine, as it may be."

Nico straightened up. "What are we looking for?"

She regarded the glasses. "I started a trial to test the effects of using different barrels to age Chardonnay. St. Isadore wine is known for being buttery and oaky, but consumers are trending toward brighter, crisper flavors."

Nico nodded. "Got it. Gabi mentioned Dellavina is also evolving its flavor profile."

Marguerite suppressed her eye roll. Of course they were; Dellavina and St. Isadore had similar Chardonnay styles. But when Casper had been at St. Isadore, he'd pooh-poohed all her suggestions.

"All the wines came from the same lot," she continued. "The first sample was aged in a five-year-old French oak barrel. The second one, in a new American oak barrel. The third one, I used a hydro barrel, which means water was used to form the staves instead of fire. And the fourth is the Chardonnay we're bottling now."

Nico leaned forward. "Where do I start?"

"Start with our current wine. Then let me know which sample you think would push St. Isadore in the right direction."

They picked up the glasses and began tasting, their conversation relaxing into jokes and laughter as they compared notes. Marguerite was in the middle of telling Nico a story about one of her biggest mistakes in winemaking "—and that's why you never add a large amount of yeast too quickly to an already fermenting tank—" when she looked up and saw Evan in the door, watching them.

She wasn't sure how long he had been there. He looked tired; even from where she sat, she could see the deep grooves worn into his cheeks and how the corners of his mouth drooped. But he was still more attractive than any human had the right to be, with his button-down shirt open at the throat to reveal a triangle of skin and his jeans seemingly tailored to show off his narrow hips and well-muscled thighs. Then their gazes caught and held, and everything else disappeared. "Hi," she said slowly.

He nodded. "Hi."

She could get lost in his eyes.

Nico stood. "I'm going to be late. Thanks, Marguerite."

She snapped out of Evan's spell. "You didn't—"

"Two is my choice," he shot back, and pushed his way past Evan.

Evan stared after him. "Good to see you, too," he called.

"He does have a date," she offered. "At La Blanchisserie."

"La Blanchisserie? Didn't know I paid him that much."

"He's been invited to dinner." She lowered her voice to a stage whisper. "By Gabi's parents."

Evan crossed the room and dropped into the chair that Marguerite would always think of as his. "Sounds like you, at least, are making headway with him. Good work."

She cocked her head and gave Evan a side-eyed look through narrowed eyes. "Pretty sure that isn't my job." She paused and added, as much for her sake as for his, "Boss."

"So, fill me in. Where are we on the Global Leader Summit event?"

They discussed the plans, locking down decisions that required his personal approval. The party was taking shape nicely thanks to

Aracely's meticulous planning, so Marguerite was startled when she glanced up and found Evan frowning. "Anything wrong?" she asked.

"How did you get Nico to laugh like that?"

She blinked. "I talked to him. I told you, you should try it."

"I've never heard him laugh like that before."

Never? She frowned. "It was a pretty normal laugh."

Evan rose from the chair and closed the door to her office, then started to pace around the room. "You may have noticed Nico and I aren't close."

"I think it's safe to say the entire winery staff has noticed. Probably most of Northern California."

"Right." He ran a hand through his hair. "This is the first time Nico and I have spent extended time under the same roof."

"The first time? What about when you were kids? Although it's obvious there's a big age gap."

"The last time we lived together, he was a

baby. I started college at seventeen. I was out of the house around the time he turned two."

"But what about holidays? Summers? Surely you went home to see your parents."

He stopped circling the room and stood so still, that for a second, she was tempted to wave her hand under his nose to see whether he was breathing or had been turned to stone. "My parents died in a car accident the start of my sophomore year."

She gasped. "I'm so sorry. For you and Nico."

He suddenly looked very young, and very broken. She yearned to reach out and comfort him. But although their friendship had settled into a comfortable rhythm and they spoke every night, that was a boundary neither of them crossed. They were careful not to touch each other. "I can't imagine how hard that must have been. For both of you."

He shrugged, his expression settling back into the Evan she knew. The Evan who would rather joke or retreat into bluster than admit he was an everyday mortal with emotions. "Save the condolences for Nico. He lost his parents when he was five. I'd already started my first company out of my college apartment."

"Eighteen is still young. You must have been devastated." She would've been if she'd lost her parents at that age. She had her differences of opinion with them, and they certainly didn't understand why she felt so strongly about Napa and the family wine-making heritage, when they couldn't wait to get out and move to Arizona, but she loved them deeply.

"I was running a business." His tone kept any emotion trapped under its surface. "A business I later sold for nine hundred thousand dollars. Pretty good money for someone in college."

She resisted pointing out even successful student entrepreneurs were allowed to mourn. "And Nico? What happened to him after you lost your parents?"

Evan resumed pacing. "My maternal grandparents raised him." He turned his flat gaze on her. "He had a good life."

She wasn't sure if he was trying to convince her, or himself. "I don't doubt it. But why did you say this is the first time you've lived under the same roof? Didn't you visit?"

He kept his head turned from her as he continued to treat her office like an oval track. "Sure." Another turn around the room. "I went to his high school graduation."

She didn't say anything, just watched him.

"I couldn't take time off," he said after three more revolutions around the room. "I sold that company and moved to California and then began and sold three more. Each more lucrative than the last. But each requiring hundred-hour workweeks." He turned back to her, his gaze holding hers hostage. "I sent my profits to my grandparents. Nico wanted for nothing."

She nodded, her throat too tight to speak.

"He had a good life," he repeated. "But then last year—" he balled his fists at his sides "—he flunked out of college. Stopped going to classes. My grandparents didn't know what to do. I stepped in."

"Do you know why he stopped?" she finally managed.

"It wasn't partying or drugs. He drinks but not to excess. And before you ask, he didn't break up with anyone so it's not 'heartache.'" He made air quotes around the last word.

She ignored his derisive snort at the thought of suffering from a broken heart. "Many find college isn't the right fit. You dropped out, too, right?"

Evan laughed, a bark devoid of mirth. "I dropped out to run a company. He flunked out without a plan. When I asked what he wanted to do, he said he wanted to be paid to drink wine. So here we are." He finally stopped wearing a path in her faded rug and pulled out her guest chair, settling his muscled bulk in it. "Tell me how you got him to laugh."

"Evan, I…" She didn't know what to say. Didn't know what the current state of her relationship with him allowed her to say. Her heart squeezed as his hazel gaze lasered in on her, as if she were a glass of water and he was stranded in the middle of the desert. "How I got Nico to laugh isn't the issue. You need to learn how you can make him laugh."

"I've tried. He rolls his eyes at my jokes."

"Because your jokes make dad jokes seem edgy."

He scowled at her, but she was glad to see a glint of humor return to his expression. And something else. A light of appreciation she both wanted to bask in and was afraid of exploring too much. She dropped her gaze and it landed on the wine aroma kit. "One of the reasons why I love working in wine is because of my family. We've been winemakers for generations. What about your family?"

Evan shrugged. "My mom was a teacher. My dad owned an auto shop. We don't have a family trade."

"What about hobbies? Do you and Nico share any?"

Evan's blank stare returned. "I don't have hobbies. I work."

"You…" She let it pass. "What about taking up Nico's interests? Nico and I get along because we share an appreciation of wine. I could teach you about it."

He smirked. "I prefer beer."

She gave him a mock frown. "I've noticed." She indicated the box. "Nico just returned this aroma kit. It's a tool used for training people's noses to identify different scents found in wine. Want to try? At least you'd have something to talk to Nico about."

His gaze sparked to life. "How does it work?"

She opened the box and chose six small vials, uncapping one before passing it across the desk to him. "Take a sniff. What do you think it is?"

He inhaled deeply, then coughed.

"A sniff," she said.

"Right." He tried again. "Um…strawberries."

She smiled. "Correct." She took it back from him and handed him another. "Now this one."

He waved it under his nose. "It's the same one. Strawberries."

"No. Although it's also a fruit."

He put his nose closer to the vial and then shook his head. "This is a trick, right?"

"The differences can be subtle. I promise, not a trick."

He leaned back in his chair, his gaze catching hers. The dark gold flecks in his eyes glowed in the late afternoon sunshine streaming through the windows. "Maybe it's because when I'm with you, all I recall is how your hair smells of strawberries."

She struggled to find her best schoolteacher voice. "You're supposed to be concentrating on the scent I gave you."

"Sorry." He lifted the vial to his nose again, then put it down and gave her a slow, crooked smile. "Still strawberries. My favorite."

Only Evan Fletcher could make a simple summer fruit sound oh-so-tantalizingly dirty. "Perhaps your sense of sight is overwhelming your sense of smell."

"Are you suggesting I close my eyes?"

"Would you keep them shut?"

He thought for a second, then his smile widened as his gaze traced the contours of her face, causing heat to rise in her cheeks. "No."

She stood up, thankful her knees still possessed enough structural integrity to hold her weight. "I might have a better idea. It's after five o'clock, right?"

Evan frowned. "It's almost six. Why?"

She opened a cabinet. If she wasn't mistaken, Linus had stored fabric wine bags for use when giving impromptu gifts...yes. She pulled out a black velvet bag and a length of satin ribbon, then held them up for Evan to see. That means it's after work hours. Or maybe I should give you a letter of resignation first?"

He watched her through hooded eyes. "You're fired until tomorrow morning."

She laughed. "Good. Because blindfolding the boss definitely violates the employment contract." She stepped to his side and placed the velvet against his eyes, tying the ribbon to keep it loosely in place. Her fingers brushed the rough stubble of his cheeks, the silky softness of his hair. She held her breath so he wouldn't hear it shudder and then stepped back. "Can you see?"

The makeshift blindfold only enhanced the curves of his well-shaped mouth, threw into relief his chiseled jaw and sharp planes of his face. "No. Let me have the scent again."

"I'll hold it for you." She placed the vial under his nose. His right hand came up to hold hers steady, his touch warm and firm. She swallowed. "Anything?"

He inhaled, then exhaled. His breath wafted over her skin, causing a shiver. "Still strawberries. And maybe sugar cookies?"

He was describing her. Her shampoo. Her body lotion. "You're peeking," she accused.

"No," he rumbled. "But your skin smells of cookies. I like it."

His voiced caused tremblors deep in her belly. "It's vanilla. But if you're not taking this seriously…"

"I am. I'd like to see you tell the difference between the scents." His hand was still cupped around hers. His grip changed, his thumb rubbing ever so slightly against the sensitive skin on the back of her hand.

She got her breathing under control. "Please. Part of my job is identifying aromas. I could identify all the scents in a kit like this in elementary school."

His beautiful mouth quirked into a half smile. "Show me."

In response, she untied the ribbon and pulled the velvet bag away from his eyes. The kaleidoscopic mix of green, amber and russet was even more mesmerizing than earlier. It took her a second before she remembered to straighten up.

"Turn around." Evan stood, took the bag

and ribbon, and re-created the makeshift blindfold on her.

The velvet was soft against her skin, the nap of the fabric tickling her eyelids where the ribbon held the bag in place. Evan guided her to the guest chair, the heat of his hand on her arm burning through the thin fabric of her blouse.

"I'm ready," she said. For what, she didn't know and couldn't name. She leaned forward, only to realize she was straining against a restraint that didn't exist. The blindfold really did transform how she processed the world around her. Without sight, her ears filled in the details of the scene: the clack of glass as Evan picked up various vials and placed them on the desk, the soothing, regular sound of his breathing. Then he was next to her, the air thick with his presence even though he had yet to touch her.

"Here."

Anticipation caused her stomach to squeeze. He picked up her hand, and the brush of his skin against hers made her nipples pebble even though all he did was place a cold glass vial in her fingers.

He guided her hand with vial up to her nose—

She sputtered and frowned in his general direction. "Horse sweat? Really?"

He took the vial from her. "I'm sorry. That was for me. I'm fascinated to know what horse sweat smells like. I'm even more fascinated why wine smells of horse sweat."

She laughed, unsure whether to be disappointed or relieved that the spell was broken. "The scent is caused by a type of wild yeast called Brettanomyces or Brett for short. It's found in red Côtes du Rhône, or it could be a sign something is off in other varietals—" She stopped. The atmosphere in the room had changed. "You're silently laughing at me, aren't you?"

"Believe me, laughing is the last thing I'm doing."

His rough whisper sent a rush of slick heat between her legs. "You glow when you talk about wine, did you know that?"

He reached for her hand, his warm fingers curling around her, guiding her to hold another cold glass bottle. "What about this one?"

She sniffed. "Bay leaf."

His chuckle was more vibration than sound.

"Now who's using their memory instead of their sense of smell?"

"It's bay leaf, Evan."

He leaned closer to her, the molecules in the air charged with his presence. "Are you so sure? My aftershave is bay leaf."

She laughed. "No, you smell of basil. And lemongrass." Not needing to see Evan to know where he was, she reached out, picked up his wrist and brought it to her nose. She closed her eyes, the better to learn him, grateful he couldn't see the pleasure on her face. "And here—" she traced his skin, identifying the ridges and valleys marking veins and tendons "—cinnamon and cloves, with a touch of orange. You used the soap sold in the winery gift shop."

Evan was still, only the pulse in his wrist beating against her fingers. She dropped his hand, panic starting to rise. She'd given herself away. Now he knew she was as keenly aware of him as he appeared to be of her. Only he was flirting for flirting's sake and she was...not flirting. She was a terrible flirt, in fact. She was incapable of keeping her emotions separate from her words and actions. Look what had happened when she tried to dissipate the tension between them by kissing him before signing her contract. The awareness only continued to build…at least on her side.

She was attracted to Evan. It wouldn't take much to fall for him, head over heels. But experience had taught her when she let others into her heart, she ended up shut out in the cold. She would not make the same mistake again. Especially not with her future at St. Isadore on the line.

Reaching up, she yanked off the blindfold and blinked as her eyes adjusted to the light.

"So," she said brightly, rising from the chair, "do you want to take the kit home? Practice on your own?"

He shook his head, his gaze unfocused. "Thank you, though. You definitely made me appreciate my sense of smell."

"Anytime. That's part of my job, after all. Teaching others about wine, that is. A good winemaker should always be able to explain their process and describe what others are drinking." She was babbling. Anything to pretend the scent of his skin didn't cause a rush of warmth deep in her belly. Anything to get back to a state of normalcy between them. "Do you think this will help you with Nico?"

He shook his head slowly. "No. Definitely not."

"Oh." She felt deflated. "It was worth a try—"

"I don't think Nico would appreciate it if I rhapsodized about how his skin smells." Evan grinned, his gaze devilishly appreciative. "But I enjoyed it. Very much."

The heat between her legs blossomed. She leaned on her desk for support. "Glad you didn't think it was a waste of time."

"Except I still don't know what horse sweat smells like."

She indicated the kit. "You can learn."

"Next time." His expression sobered. "Thank you, by the way. For being concerned about Nico. For wanting to help."

She smiled at him. "Of course. It's easy to care about him." Acting on impulse—acting as she would for any friend—she leaned up to kiss Evan on the cheek.

He turned his head at the last second. Their mouths met. His lips were firm, hard, and then he opened his mouth under hers, and all was warmth and wetness. The impact rocked her, sending her several steps back.

Too late, she realized what she'd done. She'd crossed the line. She'd touched him.

She'd kissed him.

Her hand flew to her mouth in shock. "I'm so sorry—"

He shook his head once, twice, in brisk, precise movements. Then he reached out and drew her close, his hands closing on her waist. "Strawberries and vanilla," he ground out. "You taste like you smell."

She got her breathing under control. "You don't taste of cinnamon and basil. Thankfully."

"Huh. Maybe you should try again. Make sure you're getting the right notes. That's the correct term, isn't it? Notes?"

He wanted to kiss her again? Every nerve ending screamed "yes!"

"Notes are very important. You're right, it would be a shame to miss them."

He didn't require another invitation. His hands tightened on her waist, drawing her against him. She wound her arms around his neck, daring to press even closer. Then she raised her head to his, eyes closed, lips parted, anxious for the urgency of his kiss.

But he took his time. His mouth landed everywhere but on hers: on her cheekbones, along her jawline, gentle as goose down on her eyelids. He lingered on the stretch of her neck, on the sensitive area behind her ear. He used his lips and his tongue and the scrape of his beard, lighting fires wherever he roamed, building a conflagration deep inside her that demanded more, now, here—

Something buzzed. Something had been buzzing, she slowly realized. Evan must have heard it, too. He lifted his head, his gaze black and unfocused. "Phone."

Her heart raced as if she'd just finished a triathlon. She found enough air to gasp, "Not mine."

"Mine." Keeping one hand on her waist to

hold her to him, Evan reached into his jeans pocket and pulled out a sleek smartphone. He answered with a curt, "Yes?"

Marguerite couldn't hear the other end of the call, but whoever it was didn't seem to be bearing good news. Evan let go of her and stepped away to the farthest corner of the room to finish the conversation.

She turned away, both to give him some privacy and to try to return some semblance of order to her hair and clothes. Her shirt was untucked, her hair mostly down instead of up, and she was missing a shoe although she couldn't remember how it had come off her foot. She'd probably kicked it off when she wound her leg around him…

Evan cleared his throat and she glanced up from her search for her shoe. He, too, had tidied up his appearance, although his dark curls looked far more windswept than when he'd first showed up in her office. But his shoulders were rigid and his jaw set, while apology was evident in his gaze.

"We need to talk about what just happened but—" She knew the look on his face. "You need to go back to the city even though you just got here."

"We're having ongoing issues with one of our suppliers and the CEO is unexpectedly flying in. If I leave now, I'll be there in time to have a nightcap with him, and then Luke arranged a last-minute weekend of golf at Pebble Beach. I'm sorry. Can I call you later?"

She nodded. "What about Nico?"

"I'll talk to him."

She threw him a look from under her eyelashes.

"I will," he insisted. "Wild horses can't stop me."

"Since untamed equines are in short supply in Northern California, that's a pretty safe promise. Medevco, on the other hand…" She smiled, to take any sting out of her words.

He rolled his shoulders a few times. "I know. If we can straighten out this issue, then—"

"You'll need to make Nico a priority at some point." She touched his right hand with hers, and he stilled under the contact. "If you want to get to know him, that is," she finished.

He nodded, but she wasn't sure if her words had reached their target. "Can you continue to look out for him?" he asked.

"Of course! Besides, Nico reports—oh." She smiled up at Evan, her expression steady even as his fingers caressed her knuckles, her insides melting anew. "I guess he doesn't report to me."

"Right. You're re-hired as of this moment." Evan squeezed her hand one more time, then he let go.

"I have to run. But you and I—"

"No buts. And, honestly, you don't have to gird your loins for a big conversation. You and I are good." She paused. "Boss," she emphasized.

"Boss." He considered for a minute. "I guess that means no goodbye kiss?"

She burst out laughing. "Go. Drive safely. I have my own work to finish."

But after he left she sat motionless at her desk, her thoughts tumbling after each other, like kittens playing in a box, until the sun had long vanished and darkness covered every inch of the room.

Her mind could lie to itself. Outside of work, she and Evan were friends. Friends who found each other attractive and occasionally kissed, but it didn't mean anything.

Her heart knew better.

Six

Marguerite closed her eyes and leaned under the shower's spray, enjoying the leisurely start to her Saturday. Then her eyes flew open, and she turned off the water and stuck her head outside the curtain. Was that…the sound of her front door opening and someone coming up the stairs? She was sure she'd locked it. What the—?

"Hello?" Aracely called. "You here?"

Marguerite exhaled, the adrenaline surge receding, though part of her wished she'd heard a certain male voice instead of her best friend's. "You scared me! I almost regret giving you a key," she called back, and then quickly dried off before slipping into a robe to greet her guest. "You better have brought coffee after nearly giving me a heart attack."

When Marguerite got to the kitchen, she saw Aracely standing by the kitchen table, holding a carrier tray with two cups of coffee in one hand and a white paper bag in the other. "And freshly baked doughnuts."

"I take it back. You can keep the key as long as you want." Then Marguerite frowned. "But why are you here? I thought you had an early morning meeting with a client." She took the bag from Aracely and sat down.

Aracely took the chair on the opposite side of the table. "I do. But I want to make sure I heard you correctly on the phone. You kissed Evan last night, and then he ran out the door? Do I have that right?"

Marguerite paused, a chocolate cruller halfway to her mouth. "And good morning to you, too."

"This is not normal boss-and-employee behavior."

Marguerite put the pastry down. "Did I miss a holiday? Is today Obvious Day?"

"No, it is I-care-about-my-friend-and-want-to-make-sure-she-is-okay day." Aracely's dark brown gaze met hers. "Are you okay?"

"Of course. Why wouldn't I be?"

Aracely crossed her arms over her chest, her expression the definition of skepticism.

"It's all good. In fact, yesterday I received this month's wine quality analysis from the lab, and everything looks great. It's such a relief since I wasn't sure—"

"And what did the analysis of the kiss with your boss say? Panties melted or merely socks knocked off?"

Marguerite choked on her coffee. "I told you, he fired me before we kissed. Technically, he wasn't my boss."

"Right. The game you two play. Technically, the game does not change reality. You know this, yes?"

"And we're back to Obvious Day." Marguerite bit an end off the cruller. "I know that. It just…"

"Makes it easier to not have a conversation."

"I told him we didn't need one. And we don't. Yes, he signs my paycheck and I like him—"

"Enough to kiss him several times—"

"Twice. But we both know it's not going to go any further." Marguerite put down the rest of the doughnut. She couldn't really taste it anyway. "He's still figuring out his relationship with Nico, and he thinks parking Nico here at St. Isadore is the solution. It's not, but he has to learn that for himself. But it's obvious his first priority is his company and the Silicon Valley business scene. And I'm not leaving St. Isadore."

"What if he sells it?"

Marguerite stared at Aracely. "What do you mean?"

Aracely shrugged. "You said it yourself. He bought St. Isadore as a place to put Nico while he is busy elsewhere. What if circumstances change and Nico does not stay here? Evan would sell it, no?"

"He bought St. Isadore to be a going business. Plus, there's the event. You know, the one you've been hired to plan."

"But is that not what you said he does? Sells his companies?" Aracely put her doughnut down. "Have you made any progress in finding the ledger?"

"No. I've searched the winery from top to bottom several times now. And I doubt it's in the owner's residence. I looked there after Linus died and besides, he never took business documents out of the office." Marguerite shivered despite the apartment's warmth. Evan wouldn't divest St. Isadore. Would he?

If only she had found the ledger. She knew she should have demanded a signed agreement from the beginning, but Linus prided himself on his old-fashioned values. He insisted his word was his bond and she'd had no reason to doubt him until…well, until she did. It hurt to believe he took advantage of her good faith, even going so far as to create a record, but with no intention of following through and turning the vineyard over to her.

She could still hear the jeers of Linus's great-nephews. Why would he agree to give his young female assistant ownership of the winery's premier vineyard? If Marguerite wasn't paid a fair wage for her services while Linus was alive, that was her problem, not theirs.

If the ledger hadn't shown up by now, it probably never would. Which meant Linus threw it away or otherwise destroyed it. Tears pricked her eyes.

She took a sip of coffee and decided to change tack before her memories led her deep down a disquieting rabbit hole. "Have you spoken to your family about staying in California instead of returning to Santiago?"

Aracely laughed. "Perhaps the reason I know you need to have a talk with Evan is because I am avoiding my own with my parents."

She rose from her chair. "I have to run. Talk later?"

"Of course. And thanks. For everything."

"*Claro, po.* Always." She waved and left the apartment.

The room was still after Aracely left. Too still. And Marguerite's thoughts about Evan came roaring back.

It was clear their current status was unworkable. For her peace of mind, if not her peace of libido. As she saw it, there were three choices moving forward. One, she quit working at St. Isadore, for real. Two, Evan stopped coming to St. Isadore. Three…they had that conversation after all and established new ground rules, as it was obvious the original rules would continue to be broken every time they were alone together.

The first option was out. She loved working at St. Isadore. And now she had far more responsibility than she'd had as Linus's assistant. She called the shots when it came to winemaking, now that Casper was gone. Evan gave her free reign to be as creative as she wanted to be. He may hold the purse strings, but when it came to the winery, she called the shots.

She doubted Evan would agree to the second option. Nor did she want him to.

That left the third. But while she was excited—well, excited and scared—to explore more fully the chemistry that exploded every time Evan was near, she was petrified to tell him her entire history with St. Isadore. Would he suspect her interest in him was driven solely by the prospect of material gain?

She'd like to think not. But then, once upon a time she believed Casper was a trusted mentor and Linus supported her aspirations. She was wrong on both accounts. Did she dare trust Evan? Not only with her future and her family's legacy, but with all of her?

Maybe she didn't need to own the vineyard to fulfill her ambition. Maybe what she had right now was enough. Enough that she could still achieve her long-cherished goal of restoring the Delacroix name in winemaking and, perhaps, create a new dream. One that involved Evan Fletcher, his dark curly hair and broad shoulders and firm lips she wanted to kiss for hours on end and…

She stood up. She should get dressed and start her day. She didn't need to puzzle everything out right away. Evan was in San Francisco and would probably stay there until the following weekend. She had plenty of time to—

A rap at her front door interrupted her thoughts. "Now you knock?" she called, crossing to open the door. "Why not use your key—oh."

Evan stood on the front step. She drank in his appearance. He wore khaki trousers and a hunter green button-down shirt that turned his hazel pupils to deep jade. But lines of exhaustion furrowed his forehead.

"I thought a knock was more polite." He glanced at her, then quickly looked away toward the colorful potted plants that lined the courtyard. "Sorry. I should have called first."

"I thought you were Aracely. She was just here." She clutched her robe closed at the throat. Why was he at her apartment? On a Saturday morning?

He nodded, scratching the back of his neck, his eyes still averted. "This was probably a bad idea. I'll go, give you your privacy."

"Wait—I thought you were playing golf this weekend. With the supplier. Is something wrong?"

"No. Yes. I mean, I was supposed to play, but…" He took in her bare legs, his gaze lingering on the sash loosely tied at her waist. "After yesterday and we… You know what? Let's discuss it later."

They could. They could talk in her office on Monday. She could offer to quit or he could fire her temporarily, although Aracely was right. The game didn't change reality.

Or she could put the third option she had just been mulling into motion. Now.

She let go of her robe and opened the door

wider. "Come in. There are still a few dough-nuts left, and I can make fresh coffee."

"I don't think that's a good idea. Maybe when you're dressed."

"Please. You're right. We should talk. We need to set some new rules."

"Right now, with you looking that way, there won't be much talking. The only rules I want to discuss is how to break them. For good."

His words were all it took. She let go of the door, winding her arms around his neck to bring his head to hers. Then she kissed him, hard, and let go. "Great. I feel the same way. Now, will you please come inside before we scandalize the neighbors?"

He smiled for the first time since he'd arrived as he pulled her tight against him. "Nico spent the night at Gabi's, so I'm the only neighbor. Scandalize me as much as you want."

"That's the plan," she whispered against his lips. And she kissed him again. Softly this time. Taking her time. Inviting him to stay and explore, much like he had the night before. Only this time…

His lips were still, just for a second. Then he opened to her and she wasn't sure who was kissing who, who was taking the lead and who was eagerly following. Tension pooled in her center, melting her limbs, and she locked her arms around his neck so she wouldn't be prone on the courtyard flagstones.

His mouth was hot, insistent. One of his hands traveled from her waist to wrap around the back of her head. She relaxed into his hold, intent on making him relinquish the rigid control she could sense was keeping him from fully letting go. Unlike their earlier kisses, there was no reason to hold back. No need to pretend.

She rose up on her bare toes, her robe falling open, her breasts and stomach pressing against him. She wriggled, seeking out the hard ridge in his trousers. "This is what I wanted to happen the first time I kissed you."

"This is what I wanted when you fell on top of me in the kitchen," he growled, and she laughed as he nuzzled her ear, her throat. Then his hand slipped inside her robe to find her right breast, his thumb weaving worshipful circles around it, and laughter was forgotten.

"If we don't go to my bedroom right now—"
She gasped as his hand moved lower, brushing over her abdomen, trailing lightning storms in its wake—"I'm going to scream and scare anyone out in the vineyards."

He laughed against the side of her neck. "A bed might be nice." He reached around her for the doorknob. Then he frowned.

"What's wrong?" She turned in his arms and tried the door herself. "What the—? How is this possible?" But even as she asked the question, she knew how. She hadn't unlocked the door from the inside. They were locked out.

"I don't suppose you have a hidden key out here?" he asked. "An open window?"

She shook her head. "I don't suppose you have your set of keys?"

"I've dreamed of being in your bed, but only if invited. So no, don't have them on me."

"Argh." She rattled the door again.

"It's okay. This is probably for the best, all things considered. I'll go to the main residence and get the key ring. Then you can get dressed, we can go out for breakfast and talk." He lifted her right hand to his mouth and pressed a kiss into her palm.

But she'd be damned if she let this encounter be swept under the rug. Let it be chalked up to "we're just friendly work colleagues who sometimes get carried away but then remember who we are."

"I've already had breakfast." She caught his gaze, insisting that he really see her. "I want you."

Still keeping her gaze locked on his, she undid the belt of her robe, letting it fall open. Then she shrugged it off her shoulders. It pooled at her feet, leaving her bare.

His gaze darkened despite the bright morning sun. In his throat, his Adam's apple bobbed.

"Did you know I'm the happiest when I'm outdoors? It's my favorite place to be." She stretched, her arms reaching to the blue sky above.

The air shifted. She could smell the change. "It's beginning to be my favorite, too," he said, his gaze drinking her in, lingering on her breasts, the curve of her stomach, the nest of curls at the juncture of her thighs.

She smiled, enjoying his reaction, and leaned up to kiss him anew. Then she pulled back slightly.

He quirked an eyebrow. "Second thoughts after all?"

"No. But before we go further, maybe we should discuss past partners? Healthwise?"

He shook his head. "Last real date I had was before I bought St. Isadore. Clean bill since."

"I haven't been on date in over a year. All good at my last exam." She kissed Evan, and he groaned into her mouth, their tongues exploring and tangling as she unbuttoned his shirt and tugged it free of his trousers. Her hands traveled across his lightly furred chest, her fingers rubbing across his flat nipples before finding the trail that led down his six-pack abs to the waistband of his khakis. Then they traveled lower and she gasped, gulping in air as she learned the size and the heat and the steely hardness contained within.

Soon his hands were helping hers and before she knew it, he had divested himself of his clothes. She stepped back, for only a second, so her eyes could enjoy what her touch already told her: it was the most magnificent erection she'd ever witnessed. Then she fell to her knees, her robe acting as a cushion, and took him into her mouth.

Intimacy came in many forms. But of all the acts possible between partners, she enjoyed this one especially. Not just because she controlled Evan's pleasure, using her mouth's heat and wetness and pressure to discover what made him gasp, what made him groan, what made him dig his nails into his palms and strain not to lose all control. Not because she could also use her hands to caress and stroke, pinch and pull, learning what combination made him moan her name as a profane prayer.

But because it was the most personal and private place to learn his scent.

Evan overran her senses, bringing them achingly alive. She ran her tongue along his length then suckled on the satiny head, marveling as he swelled even more, his harsh breaths music to her ears. His hand fisted in her loose hair, and he gently urged her up.

"My turn," he said simply, kissing her deeply while guiding her to the courtyard bench.

She'd always loved the bench. It was one of the things she'd missed most after Linus's nephews threw her out of the carriage house. Trellises of grapevines surrounded it on three sides, meeting high overhead to make an arch. It was a favorite place to read or day-dream or even take a nap.

But when Evan tugged her down to sit on the bench, then knelt before her, using his mouth…

Dear heavens, his mouth. His talented, wicked, relentless mouth. He lapped and en-circled and sucked, following her gasped directions, learning her cues, varying the rhythm and intensity, demanding she soar higher, faster. She tried to hold back, to savor the unreality of the moment—this was Evan between her legs, Evan worshipping her with his tongue, his fingers—but the pressure kept building and building until she had no choice but to come apart, every molecule fizzing and sparking.

Evan guided her through the waves, gentle now, slower, and when she could finally open her eyes, he was there, holding her, gathering her into his lap as he sat on the bench, his shirt as his cushion. He had the most enormous, self-satisfied grin on his face.

"Proud of yourself, aren't you," she muttered, but she was aware she probably wore the same expression.

"You have no idea," he breathed in her ear.

"I hope you have a condom in your wallet." She snuggled against his chest, the sunshine warm on her bare back.

"As a matter of fact—"

The sound of a car's tires on the gravel drive leading to the carriage house penetrated the fog of pleasure blanketing Marguerite's senses. She hopped off Evan's lap. "Car. Someone is here."

He immediately understood. Bending down, he handed Marguerite her robe and then pulled on his trousers. He had one shoe on and was searching for the other when they heard the gate to the courtyard opening. Marguerite sprang in front of him to intercept their guest.

Aracely came around the corner, her gaze locked on her phone. When she looked up, she froze in place for a minute, then gave a tiny smirk that gradually grew to encompass her entire expression.

"Hi," Marguerite said, begging Aracely with her gaze not to mention the obvious. "Meeting over so soon?"

Aracely cleared her throat. "Did I leave my portfolio here this morning? I seem to have misplaced it. Hello, Evan."

"Hi," he returned, putting his second shoe on.

"I don't think you left anything. Or at least I didn't notice," Marguerite said.

"You do seem rather…preoccupied." She glanced at the door and raised her eyebrows in a question.

Marguerite continued to stare her down.

"May I look for it?" Aracely said. "Inside?"

"Oh, sure." Marguerite exhaled. The key. Aracely had a key. "Be my guest."

Aracely's narrowed gaze ping-ponged between Marguerite and Evan. "I will," she said slowly. "I will be inside for fifteen minutes."

"Okay," Marguerite agreed. "Take your time."

"The time is not for me. It is for you, so you

know how long you have to make yourselves more presentable." Aracely swept past them and unlocked the door. She turned around before entering. "There are socks underneath the bench and what appears to be boxer shorts in the trellis."

Aracely shut the door behind her with a decided slam. At the sound, the nervous giggles Marguerite had been struggling to contain broke free, and she collapsed with laughter. Evan joined in, his strong arms holding her up when she would have melted to the ground, and the courtyard rang with mirth.

"This was not how I anticipated my morning to go," Marguerite finally said, wiping tears from her eyes.

"I didn't anticipate it. Fantasized about it, maybe. But the reality was better."

Marguerite swallowed the last of her laughs and straightened up. "So. Um. Door is open," she finished.

"I see that."

She pulled her robe tight around her and tied the belt with a double knot. A ridiculous move, considering what they had just been up to. But she appreciated the armor, flimsy though it may be. "I can make the coffee I offered earlier."

"Marguerite." Her name was both a caress and a warning.

She glanced up from the contemplation of her bare feet to catch his gaze. She read— oh, she read so many things in his eyes. Desire and hope and happiness, but also not a little trepidation. It matched the apprehension threatening to swamp her stomach. "Yes?"

"About that conversation." He retrieved the missing articles of clothing and stuffed them in his pocket. "I've been thinking about next steps."

Her heart began to race again, but this time not only due to his physical proximity. *Right. The conversation.* "You mean other than the one we just took?"

"Including the one we just took. You were pretty clear about not engaging in personal relationships at work. Are you okay with this?"

"Pretty sure you could tell how okay I was."

He smiled. "I mean about continuing to work together. I don't want people to get the wrong idea about us. That I coerced you into this."

She loved that he cared about her reputation. She loved him—no. She couldn't fall in love with him. Or at least, she could never let him know it. She was aware of the power differential in their relationship. Until she could prove her claim on the Delacroix vineyard, Evan was the ultimate arbiter of St. Isadore's future—although when it came to making day-to-day decisions about the winery, he ceded control to her. But if he knew how much she was starting to care about him, she would be utterly vulnerable.

"Or maybe people will say you're the victim, that I'm chasing you for your money," she said lightly. "We can't control what others think. But we're also not wrong to worry."

"Which means…?"

"Wine is big business but a small industry. We should continue to keep our distance at work and especially when we're around other people. But that's not too hard…" She reached up and kissed him, because she truly meant no sting in her next words, but he finished them for her.

"That's not too hard because I'm rarely here." His mouth twisted. "Speaking of—"

He stopped when Aracely appeared in the doorway, a leather portfolio case held high in one hand while the other covered her eyes.

"I found it," Aracely said. "May I safely exit now?"

Marguerite laughed. "We're decent. It's safe to go into the courtyard again."

"Well…define *decent*," Evan said, a devilish light in his gaze. Marguerite elbowed him in the side.

"I do not want to know." Aracely let the hand covering her eyes drop. "But Evan, if you are sticking around, at some point the three of us should sit down and go over the latest plans for the Global Leader Summit event."

"How about Monday afternoon?" he suggested.

"Monday?" Marguerite turned to him. "You're not heading back to the city?"

He caressed her cheek with the back of his right hand. "The deal we're pursuing is currently on hold. The investor I told you about, Angus Horne? He had a family emergency. I told Luke I was going to work from here until we can get back to the negotiating table."

You're going to work remotely from here?

Where is Evan Fletcher and what did you do to him?"

He shrugged; his body language was the perfect picture of casual indifference, while his gaze was anything but that. She shivered. "I want to learn more about St. Isadore and wine. Someone suggested that might even help me get to know my brother."

"I can't think of anything that would be better for St. Isadore."

"Just St. Isadore?"

She shook her head, not trusting herself to speak.

She wound her arms around his neck and kissed him in reply. As the kiss deepened and his grip tightened on her robe, she heard Aracely's departing laughter ring through the courtyard. Then Evan commanded her full attention, and her senses could discern only him.

Seven

Marguerite reclined on the new leather sectional sofa, sinking into the overstuffed cushions as she watched Evan and Nico argue over who deserved the last piece of the meat lover's pizza, ending with Nico offering to arm wrestle Evan for the spoils. Gabi caught her gaze and they shared an eye roll and head shake of commiseration over the men's antics as the match began. But Marguerite also couldn't help grinning. Evan and Nico competing to see who could cheat the most at arm wrestling was not something she'd ever expected to witness.

It was Friday pizza night at the owner's residence, a tradition that had sprung up shortly after Evan started working from St. Isadore. Nico had taken advantage of Evan's increased presence by asking for weekly meetings with Evan and Marguerite to discuss his work at the winery. They'd quickly determined the meeting required refreshments, which then morphed into ordering take-out pizza. At the first meal, Evan had brought out beer and Marguerite had recoiled in horror. But then she'd decided to use the occasions to teach Evan more about wine. He might still prefer beer, but at least now he could hold a conversation whenever he ran into another winery owner.

She still couldn't fully believe Evan had made good on his stated intent to work from St. Isadore. He spent his days holed up in his home office, emerging only to sign off on requests from Marguerite or the director of operations. But the nights...the nights, he definitely made his presence known. To her. At her apartment. On more than one occasion, taking advantage of the guest chair in her office. Even in the pickup truck Marguerite drove to meet with vineyard managers and walk the grapevines.

The memory of what his mouth and fingers had done to her under the open sky, with nothing but green leaves and budding fruit all around them, caused her to shift on the cushions. Evan glanced up from his match with Nico. When their gazes met he smiled, the devilish quirk of his lips telling her he knew what she was thinking. He always knew, but then Marguerite's thoughts were rather predictable ever since the morning in the courtyard.

"I win!" Nico shouted. Evan's arm was pinned to the coffee table.

Evan kept his gaze on Marguerite. "I had my eyes on a greater prize." He passed the paper plate to Nico then took a slice of margherita pizza for himself. "Enjoy."

His elbow came perilously close to the open wine bottle on the coffee table as he levered himself from his seated position on the rug. "Careful!" Marguerite reached down and moved the bottle. "This is good stuff."

He joined her on the sofa. "Then, we should finish drinking it."

"First, pop quiz. Why did we have the Cabernet Sauvignon with the meat lover's pizza?"

Evan thought for a minute. "Tannins," he replied. "The tannins offset the fat in the meat."

"And a fruit-forward wine like this particular Cab Sav pairs well with the flavor."

"I'm good at pairings," he whispered in her ear when the younger couple wasn't looking. "Quiz me more when we're alone."

Gabi finished consolidating the remaining pizza into one box and closed the lid. "We're meeting friends from my internship program." She patted the lid and grinned. "They thank you for the sustenance."

"Speaking of interns…" Nico drawled. He and Gabi exchanged a glance heavy with meaning.

Marguerite sat straight up. Evan's body language also shifted, from relaxed to attentive. "Something you two have to tell us?" he asked.

"Well…" Nico kept his gaze on the wine bottle on the coffee table. "I've been thinking. I like working here. With you," he said to Marguerite. "I'm really enjoying my rotation in the wine tasting room."

"I hear a but," Evan said.

"But." He took a deep breath. "Gabi is returning to Cornell in August. And the more I've gotten to know the other interns, the more I think… I need to go back to college." He grinned, if a bit sheepishly. "I really want to go back, despite not giving it my all before. I've decided I want to work in hospitality. For a big luxury chain. So I need those business classes after all."

Evan answered his brother with a grin of his own. "That's terrific."

"I'll still be at St, Isadore for the rest of the summer. And there are a lot of details to work out. I'm not sure Boston University will take me back, but I'm going to try."

"Nico can finish his general education courses at a junior college and then transfer to another four-year school, too," Gabi interjected.

"And that junior college wouldn't happen to be near Cornell, would it?" Evan teased.

Gabi and Nico exchanged another look. "A

lot of things to work out," Nico repeated. "But maybe."

Gabi looked at her phone. "We better run if we want to catch up with the others. See you both later."

Marguerite managed to wave goodbye, still struggling to process Nico's words. Evan poured what was left of the wine into their nearly empty glasses. "Cheers," he said, holding his up. "Here's to having the place to ourselves for the next several hours."

She could only blink at him in response.

He lowered his arm. "Something wrong?"

"No. I mean, what could be wrong?"

He searched her expression. "You don't think Nico should return to college?"

She shook her head. "It's a great idea. He's doing a spectacular job in the wine tasting room. Guests love him. He'd be a great restaurant or hotel manager, if that's what he wants."

"Then what is it? You're biting your lower lip."

Dammit, he always could read her tells. "It's just..." She hesitated, unsure how to put her initial burst of panic into words. "Well,

if Nico isn't here to learn the winery business…would you still need to own a winery?
We're a few years away from turning a sizable profit, and you've been spending a lot of
money on something that isn't your passion."

Now it was Evan's turn to blink at her.
"That's a new thought to me," he finally said.
"On several fronts."

"Oh? Which ones?"

"To be honest, I never dreamed Nico would
want to finish his degree. So, I haven't considered St. Isadore without him. And the
second…" He shrugged. "I spend money on
businesses to make money. Passion doesn't
enter into the equation."

"What about Medevco?"

"I want Medevco to succeed, and right now
that means a lot of long hours to put out hot
fires. But am I passionate? Not the same way
you are about wine."

"When I was eight, I announced to my parents I was going to be a winemaker." And she
would one day restore their family name to
preeminence in the field. "Of course, I had
never tasted it. But I knew. What did you
want to do as a child?"

"Make lots of money. My parents fought over bills at the end of the month. Then Nico came along and the fights got worse. Don't get me wrong, they didn't fight all the time. But the end of the month was rough, especially if my dad's customers didn't pay on time." He was silent for a moment, his gaze falling on his wine glass. "Anyway." He put it down and turned to face her. "Speaking of Medevco, Luke called just before Nico and Gabi showed up with the pizza."

Her stomach, which had started flopping about the time Nico made her announcement, now plummeted to the ground. "Angus Horne is back from his emergency?"

"Not yet, but he will be soon. We need to be ready. And Luke and I aren't agreeing on what ready means. Some discussions need to be held face-to-face." He pulled her into his arms and nuzzled her neck, his five-o'clock shadow pleasantly scraping her skin.

She laughed despite the trepidation starting to crawl down her back. "I hope you're not using the same approach on Luke that you use on me."

You're the only one I want to have full body

conversations with." He leaned back, his gaze searching hers. "I'm leaving for the city on Monday, and probably won't be back until the summit."

His pronouncement hit her harder than it should. Of course he would return to San Francisco. Medevco was his true priority.

It hadn't escaped her notice that he didn't really answer her question about St. Isadore's future after Nico left. Nor that his story about his parents placed a premium on making money from his businesses. She didn't have nearly enough money saved to buy the vineyard she was owed outright. Asking him to sell it to her for a below market price—much less give it to her a gift—seemed…crass.

"I'll miss you," she said, the words escaping her lips before she could stop them from forming.

His gaze traced the contours of her face. "Then come with me."

"To San Francisco? So close to the event?"

"You and Aracely have the party nailed down. I'm not worried. Besides—" and he grinned, that roguish expression that always made her heart beat far faster than it should

"—there are no prying eyes and ears in the city."

She grabbed her glass off the table and took a large sip, for once not tasting the spice and ripe berry note in her wine. "To be clear, Nico spends so much time at Gabi's, that's not necessarily an issue here."

He made an impatient movement. "But wouldn't it be nice not to worry? Plus, next Friday there's a charity gala I need to attend. And I don't have a date yet."

He leaned over and whispered in her ear, the low timbre of his voice causing her to shiver. "I'll leave on Monday, get as much work done as possible. You drive down on Thursday and become intimately acquainted with every room in my house. When we're tired of my place, we'll explore the city and then go to the gala on Friday night."

He did make it sound enticing. "Tell me more about the gala. Who will be there?"

"Silicon Valley types. Bay Area society types. The types that like to dress up and go to parties." He shrugged. "It's to raise money for local nonprofits, so it attracts a broad range of people."

"Wine industry types?" She kept her tone light.

"Ah." He nodded. "We'll say you're representing St. Isadore, to check out what's being served at the gala and keep tabs on the competition."

At St. Isadore, they could pretend the outside world didn't exist. Pretend they followed the new rules they established: they were strictly work colleagues from nine to five, while after hours they were friends with very specific and pleasurable benefits.

Pretend she wasn't falling in love with him.

Pretend she wasn't petrified he would decide he didn't want St. Isadore after Nico went back to college and dump it and her, leaving her back to square one yet again.

"Come to the city," he said against her lips. "I don't want to go two weeks without seeing you. You can take the time off from work. I'll arrange it with the boss." He wagged his eyebrows.

She laughed, helpless to resist. And maybe it wasn't a bad idea to visit San Francisco. To be part of his life in the city, if only for a few days. And perhaps to use the time to persuade him that St. Isadore was worth keeping, was worth his investment. "I'll have to drive back Saturday morning. Aracely and I have some last-minute meetings with vendors."

He picked up his glass and drained it before turning so he faced her on the sectional. She shifted to match his position, her light cotton skirt riding up and revealing a portion of her upper thigh as she moved. With his right hand, he began to trace abstract designs on her newly bared skin. "You'll have fun beyond your expectations."

His fingers brushed higher and she closed her eyes, the better to experience the swirling fire his touch so expertly kindled. "I can't imagine how you can exceed them when you've already set them very high."

"Let's see how high they can go." Then he kissed her, his firm mouth closing over hers and demanding she concentrate on only the pleasure he made her feel.

She gave in to his kiss, and the panic rattling her nerves was overtaken by the rising tide of arousal. Evan wasn't Casper and he wasn't Linus. She didn't need to fear having the rug pulled out from underneath her hard-fought goals again. Borrowing trouble only caused stress for the borrower.

But a tendril of trepidation curled up at the base of her spine and refused to go away.

The drive to San Francisco was both interminable and over far too soon for Marguerite's nerves. On the one hand, she would get her first glimpse of Evan's life outside St. Isadore, meet his friends, gain a deeper insight into what made him, well, Evan. On the other hand, they would be together for the first time without being wrapped in their St. Isadore cocoon.

Evan lived in Cole Valley, at the top of the hill, adjacent to Golden Gate Park. The neighborhood was a mixture of Victorian, mid-century and contemporary styles, with his house definitely falling into the last category. The sleek glass, metal and cement four-story structure stood out for its elegant if severe facade, all squared angles and hard surfaces. She marveled at it through her windshield as she pulled her car, dusty from the road, into the pristine driveway.

Using the app Evan had installed on her

phone, she unlocked the towering frosted-glass front door. Inside, the house was even more modern. And more impressive, with understated but obviously expensive furnishings that reminded her of TV remodeling shows featuring celebrity residences. No wonder he was less than complimentary about the dated—if still grand—decor of St. Isadore.

She put down her bag in the expansive main living quarters, which stretched the entire length of the second level, the floor-to-ceiling windows offering views of the city with the Golden Gate Bridge in the distance. The kitchen, with its sleek European appliances, flowed into the dining area, which was separated from the main room only by a fireplace that appeared to almost float in the middle of the room. The entire space was big enough to fit her apartment with room left over.

The sound of the front door opening made her jump. She whirled around from taking in the view, expecting to see Evan. Instead, it was woman, around Evan's age, with precision-cut hair framing her high cheekbones and piercing dark eyes. Her sharply tailored suit probably cost more than the entire contents of Marguerite's closet. "Oh, you're here already," the newcomer said. "Good."

Marguerite's heart thumped hard against her ribcage. Who was she? Where was Evan? "And you are…?"

"Didn't Evan tell you? No, of course not. Men." The woman rolled her eyes. "On the other hand, he and Luke have been busy, so perhaps it's forgivable. I'm Finley Smythe. A friend of Evan's—well, my brother Grayson is his friend, but Evan knew I was in town, and he asked me to look after you." She held out her right hand to shake.

Marguerite looked at Finley's hand but didn't offer her own. "Marguerite Delacroix. I wasn't aware I needed a nanny."

Finley smiled, displaying even, white teeth, and dropped her hand. "We're going to get along fine. And of course you don't need a babysitter. But Evan thought you might want a shopping companion for something to wear to the gala tomorrow."

"I don't understand." She'd borrowed an evening gown from Aracely. "I should be set. Evan knows that." She took out her phone to call him.

Finley shook her head. "He's in a closed-door meeting, will be until this evening. I know, it's annoying. My brother is in the same meeting, even though it's vital I talk to him about upcoming events. So, since I can't move forward until Grayson is liberated and you don't need to go shopping, want to show me your masquerade costume?"

"Masquerade? What masquerade?" Marguerite's head swam. It had been a long drive, and she was hungry, thirsty and overtired. Maybe she'd misheard the other woman.

Finley's gaze narrowed. "The gala. It's a masked ball."

Marguerite continued to stare at her.

Finley reached out and patted her shoulder in commiseration.

"Men." Several hours later, Marguerite had a masquerade costume assembled thanks to her companion's strategic knowledge of where to shop for supplies. The gown she'd borrowed from Aracely was a simple long slip of pale gold silk when on the hanger, but on Marguerite, it became a marvel of draping, emphasizing her curves. Taking her cue from the color of the dress—and her work—

she decided the theme of her costume would be champagne. Finley found a stole of pale cream chiffon in a local boutique, and a helpful assistant at a craft store attached oversized pearls and translucent baubles to its surface. When wound around Marguerite's shoulders and trailing down her arms, the decorations resembled bubbles rising to the top of a champagne flute. Smaller pearls and clear beads decorated the simple mask, and for her hair, they rummaged through the marked-down items at a party store and found a headband with a large paper champagne cork on top, left over from New Year's Eve.

Finley also persuaded Marguerite to buy cosmetics in various shades of gold, including glitter for her face and body. When they arrived back at Evan's house, Marguerite took her newly purchased bounty into the powder room off the living space to experiment with different looks. She then slipped on the dress to get Finley's opinion, which she had come to value during their marathon shopping expedition. "Ready?" she called through the closed door.

"Ready," replied Finley.

Marguerite stepped out. Finley clapped her hands. "Perfect," she pronounced.

But Marguerite didn't hear her. Her focus flew past Finley to alight on the person coming through the front door.

Evan stood in his foyer, his gaze locked on the vision that was Marguerite. He thought her beautiful at any time of day or night, seated behind her desk in her customary trousers and blouse or sporting jeans and a T-shirt covered in dirt from inspecting the vineyards. And of course, Marguerite in his bed, wearing nothing but her wicked grin and the light of passion in her eyes, was his favorite sight in the world.

But now she glowed, as the setting sun poured its amber rays through the windows, lighting her from behind. Her gown outlined her curves, the fabric almost appearing molten as it skimmed and dipped over her skin. Just fifteen minutes ago, he had been irritable and tired, thanks to a long day spent in a windowless conference room not making any progress on the negotiations. Now—

now Marguerite would be lucky if that dress stayed on her for more than five minutes.

And from the way her mouth hung slightly open, her gaze warm and welcoming, she knew it, too.

"This is my cue to go," he heard Finley say. At least he assumed it was Finley. He hadn't taken his eyes off Marguerite to confirm the other woman's presence. "I'm not going to the gala, so this is farewell. Nice meeting you, Marguerite. I had fun playing fairy godmother. I'll have to find a way to do it again." Finley patted him on the arm as she passed by. "Don't bother seeing me out."

"Bye, Finley," Marguerite said. "Thank you for everything."

"Don't let him rip the dress after all my hard work," Finley called, and he heard the front door open and close.

He closed the distance between him and Marguerite in seconds flat. But when he would have taken her in his arms, she held up a hand and stopped him. "The gala is a masquerade," she said. "Were you going to tell me before we arrived?"

"It's a masquerade? Huh." He assumed it

was black tie, like all the other galas he had to attend for business. Then he squinted at the silly party hat in her dark hair. "Is that a cork?"

"I'm champagne." She did a slow twirl, the silk of her dress lifting to show off her toned calves.

"You're intoxicating, all right." He made another attempt to draw her close, but she evaded his grasp.

"Finley will kill me if I let you destroy my outfit." She removed the headband and took off the filmy piece of fabric she wore draped around her shoulders. "Okay…now. But mind the dress. It's Aracely's."

He didn't need another invitation. He had dreamed of her mouth all day, to the point that Luke had made him the presenter so he would be forced to pay attention at the meeting. The heat and the wetness, the thrust of her tongue as she played with his, the way she bit gently, then suckled on his lower lip. He made his dreams a reality as his hands, jealous of the silk caressing the curves beneath, traced paths across her back, held her waist, cupped her rear and brought her tight against his increasingly impatient erection.

She pulled back slightly to grin at him, her lips red and swollen, her gaze hot and bright. "Hello. I take it you're glad to see me." She wriggled against him, and he had to count to ten backward before he could respond.

"Happy to continue to show you how much," he growled, but when he would have captured her mouth with his anew, she started to laugh. "What is it?" he asked.

"You have glitter all over your face," she snort-giggled. "In your hair, too. And on your shirt. I think it was on my hands."

No wonder she glowed. This close, he could see tiny metallic sparkles shining all over her, from her dark tresses to the shadowy valley revealed by the deep V neckline of her dress.

"Sorry, it's a pain to get rid of." She brushed at his shirt, leaving more glitter behind than she removed.

He caught her hands in his. "I have a plan."

He led her to the staircase that connected the main living floor with the bedrooms above and urged her to go first, admiring how her dress clung to her rear. Now he was going off script for the evening. He had a carefully orchestrated itinerary, everything planned and ordered to dazzle Marguerite. Drinks at a speakeasy bar, tiny and dark and private. Dinner at a Michelin-starred restaurant where he had arranged for the sommelier to bring out a bottle of Cabernet Sauvignon from St. Isadore as a surprise. Wandering the city after dinner while exchanging bites of handcrafted ice cream from one of the city's premier small-batch creameries. Then home, to—

Home. He'd never thought of the word as it applied to him. Sure, he owned residences. Two at the moment. But they were places to store his clothes and grab a few hours of sleep between work and meetings. He'd bought this place for its investment value, and the clean, modern aesthetic appealed to him. But it had come fully furnished and he never thought twice about changing the decor.

What would it be like to have a home, not just a house?

Especially if Marguerite were by his side as he turned off the lights each night. Across from him at the dining room table. Bustling in comfortable silence while they made meals together. Holding the hand of a little girl with dark curls who clung to his fingers with her other hand.

It was a nice vision. A good one. But homes were not for the likes of him. He needed to be able to pivot quickly, take advantage of opportunities, build his companies. He would never be a mow-the-lawn-on-Saturday kind of guy. He couldn't be and still be able to provide for Nico and his grandparents the way he wanted. The way he had to.

Then Marguerite reached the top of stairs and turned back to catch his gaze, her eyes glinting with mischief and passion. She slowly raised her hands to her shoulders and, her fingers lingering on her skin, pushed the thin dress straps down her arms. The silk slipped and fell away, revealing the perfect globes of her breasts, tipped with rosy pebbled peaks. "Which way to your bedroom?" she asked.

All thought fled. "First things first," he growled and took her hand, leading her to his bedroom suite and its immense bathroom.

She gasped. "This is bigger than my bedroom and living room put together."

He took out his phone, grimacing because his jeans were far too tight, and pushed a few buttons on his home app. The lights dimmed as the shades rolled up, revealing a wall of continuous glass and the city lights twinkling in the valley below.

Marguerite held her dress up to her chest. "Wow. But holy exhibitionist, Batman."

He crossed to stand behind her, his hands coming up to cover hers and gently urge her to let the dress fall, down to her waist, and then farther, to the heated tiled floor. "The glass is treated," he murmured in her ear, taking a second to bite, ever so gently, her earlobe. She shivered and pressed her back against him. "We can look out. No one can look in."

"Then, you're overdressed." She turned around in his arms, stepping out of the pooled dress and her panties. He helped her make equally quick work of his clothes. But when she took his erection in her hands, he gathered up his self-control and moved out of her grasp.

"Glitter," he said, and drew her to the shower that occupied the far end of the room.

Evan never had any particular fantasies about showers. They were utilitarian, meant for removing the day's grime. As long as there was enough water, showers didn't occupy his thoughts.

That was all changing.

He turned the shower on, the recirculation system ensuring immediate hot water. "Right temperature?" he asked Marguerite.

She responded by moving past him to stand under the rain-forest spray, her head back and her eyes closed as the water ran over her hair, over the tips of her breasts, rivulets dancing down the curves of her belly, hips, thighs.

He'd never seen anything so achingly beautiful.

Marguerite opened one eye. "You're wearing glitter, too," she said with a slow smile. "You should wash. All over."

He didn't need additional encouragement. He joined her, pulling a washcloth from a basket of fresh ones on the nearby counter. Then he squeezed a good amount of body wash onto the cloth from a decanter mounted on the shower's one tiled wall. "Turn around."

He gently ran the cloth over her back, soaping her skin and then rinsing the suds away. She shivered as he found ticklish spots. Then he filled his hands with shampoo and began to wash her hair, drawing circles on her scalp and letting the wet strands spill through his fingers.

Her breathing became rasps. Her hands flew out to brace herself against the glass wall, her body silhouetted by the city lights.

And she was his. Right now. He almost fell to his knees.

"You've ruined me," she said. "I am never letting anyone else wash my hair." She turned, the hard pebbles of her breasts rising and falling against him. "Let's see if I can ruin you."

She found his erection with her hands, which were slick and slippery with soap. She knew him by now, and he welcomed her knowledge, the steam and the spray and the wet heat surrounding them adding an extra dimension that caused his eyes to roll back in his head far too quickly. He wanted this to last, damn it, but it was hard to think with her clever fingers knowing just where to rub, to pull, to linger. His erection swelled to almost painful dimensions, the pressure becoming unbearable. She was going to ruin him far faster than anticipated—

He blindly reached out, found the valve controls and turned the water off. Marguerite stopped her ministrations, just in time. "What happened?"

"I want to make it to the bed," he ground out. "But first, I have an idea." He tugged her toward the shower bench and had her sit down. Then he unhooked the handheld sprayer from its holder next to the bench and turned a different switch.

The pressure was light, the temperature warm but not too hot. He sat down beside her and pulled her onto his lap, her legs straddling his. Then he pointed the stream of water at them.

At her, specifically. At the beautiful triangle of tangled dark curls between her legs and the delicate exposed flesh underneath. He held her open, finding the spot where the water pressure would be the most appreciated.

He would never tire of hearing her scream his name.

Later that night, after Evan called the restaurant and had his planned menu delivered to his door, after another courier brought some of San Francisco's best hand-crafted ice cream, after they turned Evan's bed into a demolition site of blankets and pillows, Marguerite collapsed against him. He stroked her back, luxuriating in the weight of her, the warmth, the tiny tremors that still shook her. She eventually calmed, her breathing slowing, and when he was pretty sure she was on the threshold of sleep, he settled her gently next to him, finding the covers and pulling them over both of them. She curled into his side with a sigh, her left hand resting on his chest.

Right over his heart.

He kissed the tip of her ear, intending to follow her into slumber. And that's when she spoke. Quietly, so quietly he could tell himself he didn't hear her correctly, that she was sleep-talking, that she didn't mean it. "I love you."

He stilled. "Marguerite?" he whispered, once

he had worked up enough moisture into his mouth. "Did you say something?"

"Wha...?" She blinked sleep-filled eyes at him. "I love your bed. Your sheets must have a gazillion thread count." Then her breaths turned into tiny snores. He'd always found her snores—snuffles, really—adorable, but they barely registered.

She'd said she loved him.

So maybe she didn't say what he thought he had heard. But now that the thought was in his head...it would not leave. What if she had said it? What would it mean?

After all, people said they loved all sorts of things, all the time. Baseball, for example. Kittens. His sheets. It was a strongly worded phrase of appreciation, nothing more. There was absolutely no reason why they couldn't continue as they had been, conducting business during the day and having fun after hours.

Then Marguerite shifted, her left leg tangling with his, her tousled hair tickling his skin, and his heart twinged in pleasure-pain at her expression, open and vulnerable in sleep.

He could no longer deny it. She might love his bedding, but he was falling in love with her.

This was a disaster.

When the screen on his phone told him it was 5:00 a.m., he carefully untangled himself from Marguerite and left the bed.

Eight

Marguerite awoke with a start. For a second she didn't know where she was, then she relaxed and sank back into the down-stuffed pillows. San Francisco. Evan's house. And it must still be the middle of the night since the room was so dark. She closed her eyes and prepared to drift back to sleep, her hand reaching out for Evan's comforting bulk—

No Evan.

Now she was fully awake. She turned over and looked at the clock on the bedside table. Eight o'clock? She blinked. That was well past the time she usually woke up. The last thing she remembered was closing her eyes after falling apart in Evan's arms. Well, he'd promised to blow her mind—and he had, wiping it so clean she'd forgotten where she was. The blackout shades covering the floor-to-ceiling windows helped add to the confusion.

There was a note on Evan's pillow that read simply, "Didn't want to wake you. Come downstairs when you're ready." So she showered and put on the casual sundress she'd packed, and eventually made her way to living area.

Evan sat at the kitchen table, intently focused on the open laptop in front of him. Shaved, showered and dressed in his usual work uniform of button-down shirt and dark jeans, he appeared as if he had been up for hours already. She hesitated on the threshold, not wanting to interrupt him, aware she had just literally tumbled out of bed. It was an odd feeling, as in Napa, she had no trouble making her presence known at any hour of the day.

He looked up and caught her gaze. His intense expression transformed into a grin, although it didn't reach his eyes. "Morning,

Sleeping Beauty," he said. "There's fresh coffee in the kitchen. And my housekeeper stocked the pantry with the best pastries in the city. Help yourself."

She nodded, her bright mood upon awaking starting to dim. Sex with Evan was always amazing, and last night hadn't been an exception. In fact, last night their connection seemed to be…one of souls, as well as their physical bodies. She wasn't sure what she expected from him this morning, but it certainly wasn't an Evan who looked like he barely remembered that he'd left her slumbering in his bed

But he was deep in a work crisis, so perhaps he had no choice. She walked farther into the kitchen but wasn't sure where the coffee maker was, much less the pantry. The counters were bare expanses of gray-veined, white marble, the floor-to-ceiling cabinetry finished in dark gray with no visible handles. "Um, Evan? Where is the coffee?"

"Allow me." Evan got up and reached behind her to touch what looked to Marguerite like part of the kitchen's backsplash then returned to the table and his laptop. A door, seamlessly concealed, rolled up to reveal a chrome-and-brushed-metal coffee maker, as sleek as everything else in the room. She would never have found it.

After filling a heavy stoneware mug she found on a rack next to the coffee maker, she clung to its handle. It felt good to hold onto something solid. Evan's house was gorgeous, but it felt like a stage set. Just this side of too perfect to be real.

St. Isadore's cozy if worn decor said, *People live and love and lead full lives here.* Evan's house said, *The photographer from* Architectural Digest *will be here any minute.*

The tendril of trepidation present ever since Nico had announced he was returning to school blossomed anew. She loved St. Isadore despite—or rather because of—its flaws. Could Evan?

Or would he sell it, disposing of a flawed and no longer necessary business asset?

"Hey," she said into the silence. "You're staring at your computer screen as if it's the only thing standing between you and disaster. Work causing a headache?"

She didn't mean it literally. But the more

she took in the set position of his jaw, the slightly ashy undertone to his complexion, she wondered if she had discovered the cause of his earlier distance.

"Definitely a pain, but lower. Like, in the ass."

"Sorry. Anything I can do to help?"

"Want to build a valuation model?"

"Does it involve LEGOs?"

A bark of laughter escaped him. "I'd love to see Luke's face if I walked in with a LEGO kit for our meeting."

"Then, no, I'm afraid that's the only model building I do." Her phone buzzed and she pulled it out of the pocket of her dress. "It's one of the vineyard managers." She answered, "Hi! What's going on?"

Evan watched Marguerite as she spoke into her phone, her dark blue eyes sparkling in the morning sun that streamed in from the floor-to-ceiling windows. But it was her bright smile that lit her face. Lit the room, for that matter, the sunshine a pale source of illumination by contrast. For the first time that he could remember in a long time, he enjoyed being present in the moment, not concentrating on what he had to accomplish and where he needed to be next.

Now that he had a few hours to become accustomed to last night's revelation, Evan could finally stop the thoughts in his head from crashing into each other without a trace of coherency. So, he didn't plan on falling in love with her. He didn't plan on falling in love with anyone at any time. His life was purposefully built to exclude any entanglements that might pull him off track from his goals. He resolutely stayed clear of the door in his mind marked Do Not Enter and surrounded by neon-red flares and bright orange caution cones. The same flares and cones that had blocked off what remained of his parents' car—

No. Not opening that door.

"Talk to you soon. Bye." Marguerite put her phone away and turned to him. Excitement danced in her gaze. "Veraison is starting."

"Very what?"

"Veraison." She pronounced the word with a Parisian flair. "It's when the grapes start to ripen." She opened up a note-taking app on her phone. "Let me jot down some thoughts while the conversation is still fresh in my head."

"Cool. But…isn't that what grapes are supposed to do? You look like you spotted Santa on your rooftop."

A full smirk twisted her lips. "Yes, wise guy, grapes ripen, and that's exactly why veraison is thrilling. This is our first indication of what kind of harvest we'll have this year, which will determine how much we bottle and when."

He nodded. "Got it. Your French accent is excellent, by the way. But then, it should be, considering your name."

She stopped typing on her phone and looked up. "Oh. About my name…"

He frowned. "What about it?"

She half smiled, half grimaced. "Marguerite is my middle name. My first name is Daisy."

"Your name is Daisy Delacroix?"

"I know, it sounds like a cartoon character."

"I think that's Daisy Duck."

"Same difference. Anyway, when I was a child my parents told me stories about my family's French winemaking history, and I was so enthralled I insisted on being called Marguerite. And Marguerite means *daisy*, so I am using my first name, just in a different form."

"Your parents named you Daisy Daisy?"

"Or Marguerite Marguerite," she pointed out. "But that's my parents for you. They're wonderful, and I love them, but they don't think things through all the way." There was a slightly bitter note to her last words but before he could puzzle it out, she continued, "They moved to Arizona when I was in college, where the only things they grow are tumbleweeds and rock gardens." She threw him a look from under her eyelashes. "You might like them."

He knew the expected response. The proper response. *Sure, I'd love to meet them.* Or even, *Let me know the next time they are in town.* She would probably be happy with a smile or a wink from him. Something. Anything.

But the alarms next to the sealed door in his mind started to clang, loudly. It was all he could do to nod his head. "If you think so."

A faint crease settled between her eyebrows and her gaze searched his. "Sorry. Parents might not be the best subject."

He scratched the back of his head. He was usually the one who read other people. But Marguerite was almost too perceptive when it came to him. It was part of the reason why he fell for her, despite every intention to fight against it.

He knew his strengths and his weaknesses. He excelled at building successful companies, selling them, and investing most of the proceeds in his next start-up. Now Medevco was poised to move to the next level. To go global in a way his previous enterprises hadn't. And to do more good. To provide new advances in medical technology. Better and more cost-efficient equipment. Expand their gift-giving program and ensure hospitals and medical centers in underserved communities were brought up to the same standards as their wealthier counterparts. But if he took his eyes off the prize, his goals may never come to fruition.

And buying and selling companies was how he provided for the people in his life, like Nico and his grandparents. He ensured the people he cared about wanted for nothing. That's how he kept them safe. If he took his focus off—

The alarms in his head sounded again. Louder. He hit a few keys on his laptop, not caring which letters he pressed.

"Parents. Sure. I'd like to meet yours. Someday."

"Someday." She nodded, her smile as bright as ever, but some of the light winked out of her eyes. A sharp arrow of regret hit him square in the chest.

Medevco's crisis wasn't solved, but the company would continue to be his. Marguerite was here, now, and he should spend every minute he could with her, to store up memories for when she would inevitably be gone. He closed his laptop and put it in the bag at his feet. "I'm sorry. I should never have left the bed. Not with you in it."

She lit up, a glorious glow suffusing her from within. "Bed's still there."

He fake-pondered for a minute. "True. But if I remember correctly, I promised to acquaint you with every room in my house." He stood up and crossed to where she stood, cupping her gorgeous face, reveling in the satin smoothness of her skin beneath his touch. "Let's start…" He bent and picked her up, her gasp of surprise joyful in his ear, and placed her so she sat on the table, her legs dangling off the edge. Then he knelt, pushing the skirt of her dress higher, revealing her rounded thighs, the scrap of lace covering her mound. He moved the lace aside and grinned up at her. "Here."

In the end, it was Marguerite who was delayed by work and arrived at the gala long after it started. The world-renowned chef hired to cater the Global Leader Summit wine tasting had a conflict come up with his television filming schedule and was forced to cancel. Marguerite and Aracely worked the phones from their respective places to find a replacement and negotiate the fees. Evan didn't want to leave the house without her, but Marguerite knew it was important to him to be present for the speech by his friend Grayson Monk, who was being honored by the philanthropy hosting the gala. So she sent him off, unbearably handsome in his tuxedo and plain black half-mask, and continued to nail down the details. Thank goodness for Aracely, who was a model of organizational efficiency. She smoothly swapped in the new chef's proposed menu and kitchen requirements without increasing the budget. They finished in time for Marguerite to throw on her champagne costume—foregoing the glitter—and make her way across the city to the Ferry Building to enjoy the last hour of the event.

The party was in full swing by the time she arrived, the riotous cacophony of music and laughter and conversation swirling around her as she searched for Evan among the dazzling lights, colorful decorations and glittering costumes. Finally, she spotted him at a table off to the corner, away from the dancers gyrating on the dance floor and the crowds lining up at the bar. He was deep in conversation with another man.

Her knees literally went weak at the sight of him. She'd thought the phrase was an overblown cliché but it was reality. Evan turned her legs to water. A nearby chair provided some momentary support.

"Marguerite. This is a surprise." The male voice came from behind her.

She schooled her expression to be still, to not reveal the immediate blooming of hurt and shock. And then she turned, knowing whom she would find. After all, she'd hung on his every word for nearly seven years. Until she learned he was stealing her ideas and passing them off as his own.

Casper Vos was an imposing man. Well over six feet tall with a helmet of bright platinum hair, he was easy to pick out in a crowd, which made avoiding him at wine industry gatherings easy to accomplish. She wondered that she had missed recognizing him tonight, especially since Casper was one of the few people not wearing a mask. But then, she'd only had eyes for Evan. "Casper. How are things at Dellavina Cellars?"

"Dellavina is the wine sponsor for tonight. Quite the coup for us. What are you doing here? This is an exclusive event." Being direct to the point of rude was another Casper trademark.

"I'm attending a party," she said, proud that her voice remained cool and steady. "And I see my date, so if you'll excuse me—" Casper followed her gaze and too late, she realized her mistake. Of course, Casper would recognize the current owner of St. Isadore.

"Your date?" He smiled. It was a rather unpleasant smile. "I see."

"It's not what you...we're here to make connections for St. Isadore." She raised her chin. "The winery is well on its way to surpassing its output of the last ten years. Both in quantity and quality."

"Quantity, perhaps." Casper shrugged one shoulder, a smirk on his lips. "Quality, impossible." He gestured at himself. "St. Isadore lacks...proficiency."

She knew he would eventually attack her talents and skills. Say what you would about Casper, at least he attacked her to her face as well as behind her back.

Anger joined the hurt, always a bad combination when it came to holding her tongue. "Therefore we aren't set in old, tired ways and St. Isadore has nowhere to go but up. But congratulations on your success at Dellavina. Tell me, which young winemaker are you stealing from now?"

The smirk disappeared, but only for a moment. Then it reappeared, deeper and more twisted than before. "You've grown claws. Brava. But you are still the same Marguerite. Still attaching yourself to St. Isadore's owners, still hoping they will throw crumbs your way, but always doomed to disappointment." He plucked a glass of red wine off a passing waiter's tray and handed it to her. "Enjoy some award-winning wine while you can. Until next time. I'm sure I'll see your resume floating around town again sooner rather than later."

He walked off and Marguerite immediately put the glass down. Her hands were shaking and the last thing she wanted to do was stain her borrowed dress.

To think she and Evan had been so careful not to reveal their personal relationship to anyone in Napa outside Aracely, only for to tip her hand to Casper Vos. Of all the unforeseen disasters. She needed to tell Evan. And then she should return to St. Isadore as soon as possible, do as much damage control as she could.

She made a beeline toward Evan's table, but as she came closer she realized Evan was not deep in discussion, he was deep in an argument.

"If we want to jump on this deal to maneuver Angus Horne into an investment, we have to move fast," he insisted.

"I've run my own analyses," his companion said. He was a dark-haired man, who, even wearing a half-mask, still managed to look ruggedly handsome. Luke Dallas, Evan's business partner, Marguerite guessed. "I'm not so sure we need Horne in the first place."

"We need him." Evan stared Luke down. "Horne is our best opportunity to grow and achieve maximum returns now."

Luke shook his head. "Only if we decide that's the right direction for the long-term health of the company. My numbers say we're better off concentrating on the markets we're in. We won't see the same immediate revenue jump, but it's more sustainable."

"I'm the CEO. We're entering the international market. It's not negotiable."

"Uh oh." A pretty blonde woman in a black and silver flapper dress appeared at Marguerite's side. "Now Evan has done it." She turned to Marguerite and held out her right hand for a shake. "Hi. I'm Danica. I'm married to the one doing an impersonation of a volcano struggling not to blow its top."

Marguerite shook the woman's proffered hand. "Marguerite. You're Luke's wife. I'm so happy to meet you."

"Likewise." Danica turned her gaze back to the table and Marguerite followed suit. The men seemed oblivious to their presence, intent on their argument. "Do we go in and try to diffuse the situation, or let them hash it out?"

"Do they often argue like this?"

Danica frowned. "No. Never. They usually see eye to eye. But since Evan bought the winery—" She stopped. "Not that the winery is the issue per se. I know you work there. But the purchase coincided with Evan pushing the idea that Medevco needs to grow bigger, faster. I wonder if he overextended himself." Her mouth twisted. "Or maybe the idea came first and the winery was the result. Evan is keen on bringing Angus Horne on board and Angus does like his wine. Maybe Evan bought it to impress him."

Marguerite shook her head. "He bought St. Isadore to give his brother a business to learn."

Danica laughed. "Please don't tell Nico that and give him false expectations."

"Don't worry. Nico decided he wants to pursue something else, anyway." And Evan had yet to discuss with her his plans for St. Isadore once Nico left. Casper's words rattled in her head. *Still attaching yourself to St. Isadore's owners, still hoping they will throw crumbs your way, but always doomed to disappointment.*

A slam on the table brought both women's attention back to the men. Evan and Luke were on their feet, their hands on the tabletop, their heads held low and down like bulls about to charge. "I don't like this," Danica said, and started to move toward Luke.

But then the tension broke, and the men's stances relaxed, although Marguerite got the distinct impression they were calling a time out, not a truce. Danica reached Luke's side and he drew her close, kissing her cheek. Evan looked around and, for the first time since she arrived at the party, caught Marguerite's gaze. A wide grin broke across his face. "You're here."

"I am." Her arms hung awkwardly at her side. Should she kiss him hello? Or go for a hug? Or—

"I'm glad," Evan said simply. "I missed you." And he took her hand in his and twined their fingers as if they were always meant to fit together. Her ribcage was suddenly too small to contain her heart.

Denial was no longer an option. She was head over heels in love with her boss. The man who also held the future of her family's legacy in his hands. And who gave her no indication this was anything but a pleasurable fling between two consenting adults.

Tonight, wrapped in a new cocoon of music and colored lights and fantastical costumes, she would allow herself to indulge in pretense one last time. Pretend that Casper's taunts hadn't found their target. That she and Evan had a future. That they could build a life together that included St. Isadore.

One last time, and then she would accept prosaic reality.

Nine

A week later, the wine tasting for the Global Leader Summit was shaping up to be the social event of the summer. Marguerite smoothed her hands over her dress, a simple sheath of dark crimson with long sleeves that clung to her arms until they reached the elbows, then belled into loose, flowing ruffles that covered her wrists, and made one last inspection of the scene.

Strings of crisscrossing globe lights had been installed on St. Isadore's large flagstone terrace. They would illuminate the various areas arranged for conversation and eating. Cocktail tables in two heights, chairs to match, and sleek, comfortable sofas would invite maximum mingling and conversation. At one end of the terrace, a deluxe Santa Maria–style grill had been installed, providing the guests with tri-tip barbeque and other delectable California-inspired dishes. And all of this would take place against a stunning backdrop of rolling hills lined with verdant grapevines.

The additional staff hired for the party gathered around Nico as he walked them through the order of events for the night, with Gabi by his side as his volunteer second-in-command.

Ted Sato, the director of operations, was setting up the wines for the formal tasting to be held later. Aracely, dressed in a flowing pink-and-purple-paisley caftan that had once belonged to her grandmother, seemed to float above the smooth stone floor as she ensured every detail, no matter how minor, was perfect: the flower arrangements, the position of the wineglasses on the catering staff's trays, the order in which the appetizers were to come out of the kitchen and be passed to the guests.

And the wine. St. Isadore may have fallen

on hard times during Linus's last years, when he'd refused to make changes or cede control, but the wine had always been consistently good. Not world-class, at least not in Marguerite's estimation, but pleasing to drink and accessible to a wide variety of aficionados. Most of the guests should enjoy the bottles she chose to serve. And for those who required a more challenging tasting experience, she'd brought out some of her newer wines that were ready to drink now, like the Sauvignon Blanc, and added some of her red-blend experiments that had aged enough to be opened by Evan to share as he thought necessary.

Nothing had been overlooked. Every contingency had a plan. There was no reason why her heart should be pounding in her ears one minute, her stomach aching dully the next.

Well, there was one reason. Tonight marked the end of her employment contract with Evan. And she didn't intend to enter into another one.

She'd spent her long drive from the city back to St. Isadore contemplating what to do next. She loved Evan. But she could no longer pretend. It was tearing her soul apart, to be with him, to touch him, to shudder in his arms but know she didn't have his heart.

She couldn't make him love her. But once she stopped pretending, other things became clearer, too. She would rather die than admit Casper Vos was right about her, but one of his barbs hit true. She had to stop hoping for a future at St. Isadore and to go after what she wanted.

Last week, between last-minute preparations for the party and the usual winery business, she drew up a business proposal and payment plan for the original Delacroix vineyard. She intended to present it to Evan tomorrow morning. Along with confessing how much she loved him.

Evan might laugh at her. Or be mad, or dismissive. Or he might immediately reciprocate her feelings and make her kick herself for being so scared. Whatever happened, at least she would have taken her future, and that of her family's legacy, into her own hands.

Her gaze found Evan almost immediately, his unruly hair under a touch more control than normal. He'd arrived that morning, having stayed in San Francisco the past week to, as he put it, "knock sense into Luke," who was also due at the party. She drank in his appearance. He wore a variation of his usual tech industry work uniform, but the khaki trousers were well tailored to skim just so over his powerful thighs, the fine cotton shirt was equally fitted, and the addition of a sports jacket only emphasized his broad shoulders. He raised a hand and then pointed at her, signaling for her to stay put as he walked toward her. As he drew closer, he smiled. "There you are. I've been looking for you."

Her pulse fluttered, as it always did when he was near enough to touch. She kept her hands clasped together behind her back. "What do you think of your event?"

"Stunning."

"It is, isn't it? Aracely and her team did an amazing job." The sun moved lower in the sky, its bright, golden light throwing a burnished glow over the winery's stonework and the vineyards beyond. A gentle breeze played with her hair, lifting the strands that refused to stay put in a bun. The smooth stone floor, which had seemed so cold and empty before the guests arrived, now appeared warm and intimate as people broke into small conversational groups and took advantage of the chairs and tables dotted around the perimeter. She turned back and caught Evan's gaze.

He wasn't looking at the Napa scenery. His attention was fixed on her. "Beautiful. Absolutely."

Normally, she loved it when Evan flirted with her. But acknowledging that his flirtations would never lead to anything more than the friends with benefits arrangement they currently enjoyed sucked some of the joy out of it. "Glad you approve. Of the party." She nodded at Aracely, somehow simultaneously greeting guests, whisking away empty glasses and handing out new ones. "Speaking of, I should go help her."

He grabbed her hand. She steeled her heart against the fit of their fingers. "Come join my table for the wine tasting later. Luke will be there. And you never did meet Grayson."

"Evan." She hesitated, digging deep for the resolve she'd found on her drive back from San Francisco. "I work for St. Isadore. You're the owner. This is a work event." She glanced at the terrace, now packed with faces she recognized from news articles she'd read on her phone. "Tonight, I'm your winery employee."

A shadow passed over his expression, but it disappeared so fast she wasn't sure if she actually saw it. "Sorry. I forgot. Professional. In fact, until the party is over, I'll act like I barely know you."

She laughed. "Good luck acting like you don't know your own winemaker."

"But tomorrow," he said, his voice dropping to the bass rumble that made thrills run up and down her spine, "tomorrow we need to discuss your new contract. I look forward to the part before we sign it."

"Speaking of," she started, only to be interrupted from a shout coming from behind Evan.

"Hey, Fletcher! I like your wine. So let's talk."

She peered over Evan's shoulder and saw a man, about Evan's age, grab a glass of wine off a passing tray and then veer toward them. Even without the shouting, he would still draw a second glance from her, thanks to his shock of bright red hair. He was popular, too. He barely took two steps before one guest after another came up to engage him in conversation.

Evan turned around and waved to acknowledge the shout. "Angus."

"That's Angus Horne?" she stage-whispered. "I was expecting someone…older. More established-looking."

"The older, more established people all said no to the amount of investment I'm looking for. But Angus likes risk and Medevco fits into his international strategy." Evan glanced down at her, calculations already forming behind his eyes. "I need to meet with him and Luke."

He let her hand go, but not without one final squeeze, and began to make his way toward the clump of people surrounding Angus Horne. "Until later."

"You have no idea," she muttered to herself. But until then, she had to get through the party. She turned to find Aracely, only to hear her name called. "Marguerite! So good to see you're still here."

She smiled as Orson Whitaker approached her, his wheelchair lightly humming. Owner of the Adrasteia Group, one of the largest beverage alcohol companies in the world—which included Dellavina Cellars among its brands—he and Linus were of the same generation and had run in the same social groups.

She smiled. "Mr. Whitaker. A pleasure." She grabbed a nearby unused chair and sat down next to him.

He shook her proffered hand, holding it with both of his. "Call me Orson. The old place looks amazing. I'm so sorry I missed Linus's memorial, but work took me to Europe and I only now returned for the summit. My condolences, again."

"Thank you. He would've been happy to hear your compliments, although he would have thought them naturally his due."

"Now, we both know Linus would've never approved of the barbeque. Even the strings of lights, pretty as they are."

"True. He would have said they were below the dignity of St. Isadore."

"I also hear you're doing interesting things with wine. Dellavina Cellars hired the wrong person." Orson chuckled. "Don't look so surprised. My granddaughter Gabrielle is impressed with you. And not impressed with Vos."

Marguerite raised her eyebrows. "Gabrielle… Gabi is your granddaughter? She hasn't said anything."

"Gabrielle earned her internship. She's a natural winemaking talent."

"I agree."

"Yes, it takes one to know one. But you also understand why Gabrielle doesn't volunteer the information."

"I do know something about keeping relationships quiet out of fear of people getting the wrong idea." Marguerite said, her gaze searching out Evan.

Orson nodded and turned to look over the terrace and the vineyards beyond. "Pity I didn't pursue this place when it was up for sale. I assure you Adrasteia Group would have been a better fit for St. Isadore instead of selling to Evan Fletcher. I would have given you a fair price."

"Given *me* a fair price? You mean Linus's great-nephews."

Orson swiveled his head to look at her, his

eyebrows raised. "No, my dear, I mean you. Linus was clear you should receive what you deserve."

Despite the warm temperature, Marguerite's teeth chattered as if she were in the Artic. "You must be mistaken."

"Young lady, I am rarely mistaken. Which is why I am a charter member of the group gathering here today." He looked at her closely. "I see this is news to you. Ah. Well, perhaps he thought better of it. Forgive me if I spoke out of turn." He turned his chair to leave.

"Wait—when did he say that?"

He thought for a moment. "It was the last time I saw him. Shortly before his stroke, I believe. But people do change their plans, you know." He reached out and patted her hand where it lay on her chair's armrest. "However, do not doubt he knew the value of your contributions. I may have hired Vos, but Linus was adamant you were the true talent. Not that he was about to let you go, of course. A good man, Linus was, but he had his selfish streak. Now, if you will excuse me, I should say hello to others." He wheeled away. Rather jauntily, Marguerite thought, for someone who'd just thrown a grenade into her life and shredded it.

She rose from the chair and put it back where she'd found it, leaning on its back when tears sprang into her eyes. Linus had appreciated her. He meant to upheld their bargain and turn the Delacroix vineyard over to her after all. A piece of her soul she hadn't been aware was missing clicked back into place.

He should have told her to her face, and she should have insisted on a formal agreement from the start. She'd allowed sentiment to lead instead of logic. And while it was good—oh, so good!—to learn from a third party he'd meant to keep his word, he hadn't followed through.

Still, the angry hurt that punched holes in her heart whenever she thought of Linus folded up its daggers and faded away.

"All is well?" Aracely materialized next to her.

"Huh?" Marguerite shook her head to clear it. "Yes. Of course. Why?"

"You have impersonated a statue for ten minutes."

Marguerite relaxed her shoulders, but they almost immediately sprang back to their previous position around her ears. "I'm fine. Just…thinking."

Her gaze found Evan again, standing in a tight knot consisting of Angus Horne and Luke. They were deep in intense discussion, the crowd ebbing and flowing around them like a river around a rock.

This was going to be the longest party she'd ever attended, and it had just started.

Evan sat down in the creaky leather chair and dropped his head into his hands. How had he not foreseen this? He was dealing with Angus Horne. It was a given the negotiations would not be straightforward.

He had to hand it to Angus, however. Horne loved creating chaos, but even he couldn't have known how much mental turmoil he was causing Evan.

The hour was late. The wine tasting was long over, and the cleanup crew was gone. Only the barbecue pit on the terrace, waiting to be removed in the morning, provided physical evidence the party had occurred. The guests had dispersed to the nearby summit host hotel, most of them probably asleep in order to get an early start to a weekend full of keynote speeches, exclusive roundtable discussions and chance encounters that would shape the direction of global business for the year to come. Those that weren't asleep— well, they were no doubt engaged in far more pleasurable activities than sitting in the dark in a faux Gothic library, contemplating the best choice between a rock and a hard place.

Evan had picked the library in the owner's residence for soul-searching in the wee hours of the night because it was the one room at St. Isadore that he had yet to touch, in part because the furnishings were massive and would require teams of workmen to remove—and perhaps necessitate rebuilding the entire room. The heavy oak bookcases stretched from the floor to the ceiling high overhead. The reading nooks—there were three—featured armchairs that could accommodate two people plus a good-sized dog. The desk he sat behind was solid wood on three sides, with sizable drawer pedestals.

If he put it in his San Francisco office, he'd barely have room left over for a potted plant.

And grapevines were everywhere. Carved into the crown molding. Painted on the sides of the bookcases. Woven into the rugs.

The room had nothing to do with Silicon Valley, not even a computer to remind him of tech-world wheeling and dealing. But it had everything to do with St. Isadore.

And Marguerite. Whom he'd managed to avoid ever since he, Luke and Angus had shaken hands on the outline of the deal to put Medevco on the international map.

In the past week, he couldn't shake himself of certain visions. Marguerite falling asleep on his shoulder after a long day, laughter around a fully occupied dinner table, a small child with dark curls tugging on his hand. He even began to wonder if he could make those visions a reality.

But he should have known. His life was not meant to have such things.

He should have known. His life wasn't meant for such things.

His hands would not stay still. He picked up the paperweight sitting on the desk, looking for something to occupy his fingers while his mind built and discarded one decision tree after another. But the paperweight, a crystal globe encasing a miniature version of the winery, was lighter than he'd anticipated, the smooth surface more slippery. It rolled out of his grasp and under the desk.

"Damn it." He had no idea if the object had any monetary or sentimental value. He turned on the lamps and to get a better look but the paperweight had rolled to the far corner. Nothing to do but crawl under the desk.

The desk was tall enough for him to be on his hands and knees with headroom to spare. Using the flashlight app on his cell, he reached for the paperweight with his other hand but his fingertips put enough spin on the globe to shoot it out of his grasp. He sighed and rolled his eyes, waving the phone around for illumination Then he stared.

Something white was sticking out from behind the drawer pedestal on the left side. Several somethings. The desk had been emptied before he moved in, but some items must have fallen behind the drawers and been overlooked. He reached out and pulled.

The flashlight app revealed a motley collection of flotsam and jetsam that had been shoved in drawers, fallen behind them and then forgotten over the years. An invoice addressed to the Kennedy-era White House for several cases of Chardonnay. Bills of sale for new oak casks. Faded drugstore receipts, mostly illegible. A small leatherbound ledger with "M. Delacroix" inscribed on the front. A ticket stub from opening night of the San Francisco Opera, dated 1987. More receipts—

Wait. Evan found the ledger again, using the flashlight on his phone to look at it more carefully.

M. Delacroix? As in Marguerite?

He opened the ledger and a handwritten note on a piece of lined legal-size notepaper, folded into threes, fell out.

He unfolded the paper and started to read.

Marguerite couldn't sleep. Not only was she still keyed up from the party—St. Isadore had worked its usual magic on the guests, who'd raved about her wine and Hunter Chase's food and the overall ambiance—she was acutely aware Evan was in the owner's residence, only a brisk fifteen minutes' walk away.

She hadn't had a chance to speak to him after their brief conversation on the terrace. Despite receiving two bottles to take home as party favors, many guests had asked to purchase additional wine as well as St. Isadore souvenirs. She had been pressed into service at the second cash register in the gift shop when she wasn't busy giving impromptu tours to people who requested them. Evan had seemed equally preoccupied even after his conversation with Angus Horne had concluded, dashing about the party, flashing his grin as he mingled with guests, but his gaze never finding hers. By the time she'd finished helping with cleanup, he was nowhere to be found, and she'd assumed he was having a nightcap with his fellow titans of industry or perhaps turning in early to attend the summit meetings the next day.

But the thing about revelations—like the one she'd been sitting on all week—was that they had to be shared. Casper's taunts and Orson's kind words and her own heart, demanding to be heard, were not going to let her sleep.

So when she looked out her window and saw light coming from what had to be the library, she didn't hesitate. Nico had pretty much moved into Gabi's apartment, so the lit lamp had to signify Evan's presence. She threw on sneakers and a long cardigan over her knit pajama pants and camisole and, after grabbing a flashlight on her way out of the apartment, ran down the stairs and into the main garage on the other side of the court-yard.

The quickest way to the library, she knew from her previous role as Linus's assistant, was through the secret passageway that con-nected the former stables to the main build-ing. The winery maintenance staff continued to keep the tunnels in decent shape, so she arrived on the other side of the secret door without any mishap or unwanted encounters with four-, six- or eight-legged creatures. She paused, twisting her hair into a semblance of a bun on top of her head and using the time to bring her breathing under control. Although, if things went as she hoped, she would be plenty breathless soon.

Then she knocked. "Evan? It's me."

She heard a loud thump, followed by a groan. She wrenched the door open, revealing the life-size portrait of Linus on the other side. "Evan? Are you okay?"

She blinked several times as her eyes got accustomed to the light, dim as it was. Where was he—*oh*. She blinked again, this time at the sight of Evan crawling out from under the desk commissioned by the original founder of St. Isadore. He held one hand to the back of his head.

She crossed the room, leaving the secret door open. "What happened? Are you hurt? Let me see."

But when she reached for him, he evaded her touch, retreating into the shadows as she advanced. His eyes were dark and unreadable. "I'm not imagining this. You really are here."

It was a flat statement. No, more than flat. His voice was controlled. And that scared her. Evan didn't do controlled. He bantered and, on occasion, blustered. The lack of emotion stopped her cold. "I am."

His gaze flicked away from her and he laughed, but there was no mirth in it. "Should have known. Another late-night break-in. How many times didn't I catch you?"

"I... I haven't... I saw the light on and the secret passageway was the fastest way to reach the library—"

"Of course. Secret passageway. Another of St. Isadore's secrets."

"Evan, you're scaring me. What's wrong? Did Angus say no to the investment?" It was a possible explanation for Evan's behavior. Although she doubted a business deal, even a deal that turned sour, would cause this re-action.

Ha! If only." The derision in his tone turned her from scared to petrified. "That's good, right?" She wrapped her arms around her, both to stay warm and because the atmosphere required armor of some sort. "Congrat-ulations. I know how hard you've worked."

"You might want to hold your congrats."

"He would only invest in Medevco if I in-cluded St. Isadore in the pot." Evan fell into the chair, pressing his fingers hard into his temple. He wants me to sell the entire estate to him."

Sell St. Isadore? Was she too late? Marguerite took the guest chair from its place, pulled it around to the other side and sat next to him. Her hands were numb. She didn't know if they would ever warm up. "Have you given him a response?"

"My first thought was to counteroffer." He continued as if she hadn't spoken. "Maybe give him a partial interest. Or the wine-distribution rights. Or sell him the private residence, since he kept talking about the winery's 'chill vibes' and 'potential for social,' but I'd keep the rest." He shook his head. "Something. Anything to satisfy Horne's deal requirements but maintain control of St. Isadore."

The pressure on her chest making it difficult to breath lessened. Evan didn't jump at chance to sell. Maybe St. Isadore meant something to him more than dollars and cents. She tried to smile. "It's disappointing you didn't get what you wanted from Horne right away, but this is just the opening salvo in the negotiations."

"There won't be another round of negotiations." His tone was final. And that was the scariest thing she had heard all night thus far.

She rose from her chair and started to pace along the rug. "So, what happens next? You'll sell St. Isadore to him?"

Her voice cracked on the word *sell*, but she recovered by the time she finished speaking. The thought of losing St. Isadore anew caused her skin to prickle as though punctured by thousands of straight pins. It hurt, damn it.

But it was nothing compared to the pain caused by the ice in Evan's gaze. He'd never looked at her that way—not even when he first caught her taking her wine from the owner's cellar.

"Why are you here, Marguerite?"

She blinked at the non sequitur. "I'm here because I wanted to talk to you, and I didn't want to wait until morning."

"No. Why are you here, at St. Isadore? Why did you break in that night?"

She frowned. What did he mean by his question? "I told you." She rubbed her hands together, trying to restore feeling to her fingers. "I thought the new owner would tear down the buildings, and I wanted to save the wine I made."

He scoffed and stood up. "At least your story is consistent."

"What the hell does that mean?" The anger was quick to spark, and she welcomed its warmth. Anything to counteract the wall of frost Evan had built around him. "You've known me for six months. Of course I'm consistent. I've been consistent from the moment I met you. You know that. We talk every day."

"But not about everything. Not about the things you leave out."

A hot flush settled in her cheeks. "What things do I leave out?"

He shook his head, closing his eyes as if he couldn't bear to look at her. And it was the disappointment written deep in his expression that hurt the most in a night of very sharp and deep hurts.

She swallowed. What had changed? What brought this on? Maybe…maybe he had his own revelation during the past week. Maybe he decided he, too, was tired of the pretending. True, he didn't seem upset when she saw him earlier, but that was hours ago when they were surrounded by the world's VIPs. Maybe, with the stress and anticipation of the party now over, he'd had time to think. Reconsider.

And she was disappointed in herself, too. She'd chosen to hide instead of stepping into the light, afraid to tell him how she felt because he might reject her. Afraid to trust him, allowing the way other people treated her to color her perception of him.

She took a deep breath. It was now or never. "You asked me why I'm here tonight. I came to tell you I can't keep pretending there's nothing between us but sexual attraction, and someday it will go away and we'll be fine with that. I want a real relationship. One we don't have to hide."

She stepped closer to him, so close she could lift her hand and caress his cheek. "I love you, Evan Fletcher." She smiled. "I literally fell for you from the moment I tripped over your legs in the kitchen."

They stood in the circle of the lamplight, its glow surrounding them. His gaze, which had traveled over every inch of the library except the spot where she stood, now flew to meet hers. In it she read all she could have ever hoped for, and more.

He loved her, too. His caring was as deep as the ocean and as expansive as the sky. The emotion was real and rich and rooted in his soul.

She reached for him, her hands yearning to caress, her mouth eager for his.

He stepped out of her grasp. The icy shell that had cracked open enough for her to glimpse the truth of his heart re-formed, thicker and more opaque than before.

Her hands fell away. Somehow, she kept breathing despite the hurt slamming down on her hopes and severing them like a guillotine blade.

"I want to believe you." His words barely penetrated past the metallic ringing in her ears. "Because I fell for you. Hard. I even had these dreams—" He stopped. "It doesn't matter." He turned back to the desk and stooped to pick up a crumbled letter and a small book from underneath the desk, handing them to her. "I'm guessing this is what you are truly after."

Somehow, she made herself take the things from him. Somehow, her eyes managed to focus on the top item. The missing ledger, with her name embossed in gold on the cover.

"Where did you find this? I've looked all over." Her voice was raspy from holding back tears. "But what's this letter?" Linus's signature, bold and black, was unmistakable. The date was just before he died. She unfolded the papers and started to read as he spoke.

"I asked you to hold the congratulations earlier because, as you see for yourself, they properly belong to you." He mimed raising a glass in celebration, his gaze flat. "Cheers. You're the proud owner of St. Isadore."

Ten

Once, when he was a small child and still believed in things like the Tooth Fairy and families that stayed together forever, Evan had walked in on his parents arguing in the kitchen. He was too young to understand the topic, but the memory was seared into his brain. Years later, he understood they'd been discussing money. Or rather, their lack of it. But at the time, all he knew was that his father—his tall, strong, superhero father— was crying.

The sight had shaken the bedrock foundations of Evan's young world. He cried, but his father? Adults didn't shed tears. And when his mother caught sight of him, standing shell-shocked on the threshold, she'd been so flustered she shut the door in his face. She opened it again almost immediately, but Evan had gotten the message.

Never let others see your emotions. Remain cool.

When feelings take control, calamity follows.

He'd clung to that lesson when he viewed the wreckage of his parents' car. He'd remained stoic at their funeral. His control had remained solid, even when Nico was hospitalized during high school with a fever of unknown origin, even when girlfriends left him.

Tonight threatened to destroy his perfect record.

He wasn't upset the ownership of St. Isadore might be in question. The physical discovery of the will was upsetting only because it meant Marguerite had been cheated out of Linus's bequest. A large bequest, one that would have made her life financially secure.

But he was furious—the rage lighting up his insides like an out-of-control forest fire—she'd never told him about her arrangement with Linus. Never mentioned to him she was related to the winery's founding family. He would have ensured she received her fair share. He would have made it right.

Finding the handwritten will as he was contemplating not only the future of St. Isadore but his own possible future with Marguerite was a coincidence, nothing more. But if he did give credence to the idea the universe was sentient and could speak to him, tonight would be a sign—and the sign would say he was right.

Relationships, family: they were not meant for him. His feelings drew him off course, distracted him from his goals. If he hadn't been concerned about Marguerite and her future should he sell St. Isadore, he wouldn't have been up late in the library. The paperweight would still be on the desk, not under it. He wouldn't have made his discovery. The deal with Angus Horne would be underway. Nico, his grandparents, Marguerite—he would finally have enough resources to assure everyone's financial future.

He wouldn't have this burning hole in the

middle of his chest, a sucking wound that made it difficult to breathe.

Why hadn't she told him? What else was she keeping from him?

Marguerite looked up, her eyes wide and wild. The paper shook in her hands. "I… I don't…what is this?"

"You tell me." His voice was steady, thanks to long practice controlling his emotions. "If I had to guess, it's a holographic will written by the prior owner of St. Isadore. Leaving the entire estate to you."

"I have no idea what *holographic* means."

"Handwritten will. Valid in California, if that's his signature."

"Um…" She stared at the paper. "It looks like Linus's handwriting. But… I don't… where did this come from?"

"Does it matter? The real question is if you knew it existed." He was surprised at how calm he sounded.

"No! I had no—" She stopped. Swallowed. Put the will down on the desk and smoothed it with her hands. Turned to face him. "You know I worked for Linus."

"Linus *Delacroix* Chappell," he supplied, emphasizing the second name.

Her gaze flashed. "Yes, we were distantly related. We're both descended from the original founder of St. Isadore."

"You didn't tell me."

"Why did I need to tell you?" Her hands balled on her hips. Gentle curves he loved to hold—

No. No emotions.

"It wasn't a secret." She marched over to the life-size portrait that had concealed the secret door and pointed to a nameplate integrated into the ornate, gilded frame. "Linus's full name is right here. Has been since before you moved in."

So, he'd missed it. Apparently he missed a lot of things. So much for his vaunted powers of perception. "Fine. Go on. You worked for Linus."

"We had a deal. I would be his assistant and in my off time, learn as much as I could about winemaking and the wine business. But instead of earning a full salary, I took fifteen percent, with the rest going toward purchasing the original Delacroix vineyard."

She nodded at the ledger. "That's Linus's record. You'll see I paid off the vineyard shortly before his death. You said yourself I was underpaid and that's the reason why."

He narrowed his gaze. "I bought St. Isadore from two brothers. Your name wasn't on the deed."

She sighed, her shoulders slumping. "I know. Linus was going to have the paperwork drawn up but then he died without a will, which meant everything went to his closest living relatives after probate finished. And without the ledger, his great-nephews weren't about to listen to me. They told me to leave and locked me out of the carriage house apartment. When I tried to get their attention so I could plead my case, they had me arrested for disturbing the peace." Her lips formed a trembling smile. "At least they later dropped the charges."

"The night we met. Why were you here?"

"We've been over this! I only wanted what was mine."

Right. What was rightfully hers. Which meant she would do what she needed to obtain it. Like breaking in. Or…

Or telling him she loved him.

His heart squeezed, a hard pressure that took his breath away.

He picked up the will. "Including this."

Her eyes went wide. "I didn't know."

He stared her down.

"I didn't!" she protested. "I mean, yes, I knew the ledger existed." She ran her right hand over the paper. "I had no idea he left me St. Isadore."

The last words were whispered, nearly inaudible. Her wistful expression caused something deep inside Evan's chest to twinge. He ignored it.

He'd give her one last chance to come clean. "So you didn't ask for a job at St. Isadore so you could search for this will."

"Of course not—" Her mouth closed. "Yes. I did search for the ledger. And yes, being able to search for the ledger did enter my mind when I asked for the job. But I didn't know about the will."

Her words were a meteor, creating a crater on impact. He couldn't hold her gaze.

"I wanted the ledger because damn it, I worked for the vineyard. I earned it. And it hurt to think that Linus had no intention of upholding his end of the bargain. But after— after the morning in the carriage house courtyard…" Her voice cracked, just a little. "After that, I thought I could, perhaps, build something new. We could build something together."

She huffed and picked up the will. "We're going to keep going in circles. You think this is what I want? The estate has been probated and sold. Legally, I bet this is meaningless. It doesn't matter. Not to us."

And that was where she was wrong. Because he knew his value, and it was ensuring the people in his life were well provided for. She didn't love him. Because she didn't tell him she had been cheated out of the vineyard. "No. It matters to me. You didn't trust me to make this right."

She took a step back. Her chest rose and fell several times. Then she reached around the desk, opened the drawer nearest to her, and took out a black permanent marker. She scribbled on the will, folded it up, and held it in her right hand before turning to face him.

Her gaze burned bright. "Yes. I didn't tell

you. But not because I didn't trust you. Instead, I didn't trust myself. Linus and Casper made me doubt my abilities, and I was afraid if I told you Linus reneged on his promise, you would doubt if I was capable, too."

Something inside him started to unbend. "I would never—"

"I know. But tonight? This discussion isn't about me." She shook her head, sending black tendrils falling down her cheeks. "It isn't even about who owns St. Isadore. This is about you. And your fear."

"My *what*?" Now he was back to fury. It did taste better than bitterness. Barely.

She defiantly lifted her chin and stared him down. "You're afraid to let people get close to you. You push away Nico. Now you're making up a reason to push me away. For heaven's sake, Evan, you don't have a single family memento on display in your home in San Francisco."

"My house? What does that—?" The loud pounding of his pulse in his ears made it difficult to think.

"You don't want people to see you. The real you. And you think Nico and I don't need you because you gave us buildings and businesses to run, perhaps because buildings and businesses are the only things you will allow yourself." She held out the will. He automatically reached out to take it, but she didn't relinquish her grip. "If I didn't trust you, I wouldn't have worked for you. I definitely would not be here telling you I love you. Because when you tell people you love them, you're entrusting them with your heart. And hearts are fragile." She caught her lower lip with her teeth. "Maybe that's why you refuse to trust yours."

Her hand dropped, and the will was in his sole possession. She continued to hold his gaze. "If you ever decide you deserve to be loved, for you and not for your possessions, come find me. If it's not too late."

Her words landed with the precision of a heat-seeking missile, fragmenting his worldview into thousands of sharp pieces. The shards pinned him into place, so he was unable to think or react or respond. He merely clutched the piece of paper, a reminder that the will was tangible. The will, he could deal with. He unfolded it and began to read.

In big black letters printed over Linus's handwriting, she'd scrawled, "I, Marguerite Delacroix, renounce any claim to St. Isadore and declare Evan Fletcher to be the sole owner. P.S. If you sell, please protect the staff. P.P.S. This is my resignation letter. I quit. For good."

No. This wasn't what he wanted. The winery was hers. "Marguerite, this isn't—"

But when he looked up, the library was empty. The portrait was back in its place, the secret passage hidden as if she had never been there.

Whoever was knocking on Marguerite's door wouldn't quit. Marguerite moaned and put her pillow over her ears, but it didn't stop the noise. Not that it mattered. She hadn't gotten any sleep after arriving back at her apartment following her confrontation with Evan. She wasn't going to get sleep now that the sun was well into the sky. A glance at her text messages—Evan's name wholly absent from the notifications—told her who was on her doorstep. She threw on the first clothes she found and made her way downstairs to the front entrance.

"I have caffeine. And cupcakes. I have decided doughnuts do not have enough frosting." Aracely held up a large container stamped with the logo of a local coffee shop in one, a pink bakery box in the other. "May I come in?"

Marguerite motioned for her friend to enter and then to follow her up to the kitchen. "Are you sure you brought enough?"

Aracely checked the container. "It says this contains twelve cups of coffee, so I will run out to get more in an hour or so."

Marguerite chuckled, then instantly wished she hadn't. "Ow."

"Hungover?"

"Only from lack of sleep." And crying until her tear ducts were empty. "But that's enough to cause a headache." She opened a cabinet and selected two of the largest mugs she owned. "Fill them up. Then you can help me pack."

Aracely poured the coffee and handed Marguerite a full mug. "Pack? What are you talking about? I am here to celebrate last night. The party was perfect, if I do say so myself."

"It was." Marguerite took a much-needed sip. "Ah. This is spectacular. Thank you."

Aracely took the mug away from her. "No more until you tell me what is going on."

"I... I realized I've made a muddle of my entire life. Hey, do you need a traveling partner when you return to Chile? I've always wanted to learn how to make *pisco*. What better place to do so?"

Aracely handed her back her coffee and joined her to sit at the kitchen table. "Here. I was wrong to take this away. You are not yet coherent."

Marguerite sighed. "After the party, I told Evan I loved him."

Aracely put down her mug. "Oh."

There was a wealth of understanding in Aracely's breathed syllable. "The outcome was even worse than you're imagining," Marguerite admitted.

"Are you okay?"

"I will be. Eventually."

"But why pack? He did not fire you. That would be appalling, even for—"

"I quit. Forever. I can't stay at St. Isadore."
Marguerite looked around her apartment. The
last time she moved out, she'd been given less
than twelve hours to take away her possessions. Evan wouldn't call the sheriff on her
like Linus's great-nephews had, but she also
didn't want to stay any longer than necessary.
One more crack would shatter her heart into
so many pieces, she doubted if she could ever
make it whole.

Aracely regarded her. "What about the
Delacroix vineyard? Your goals?"

Marguerite pressed her eyes shut. "When
you don't sleep, you have a lot of time for
thinking." Yes, terroir mattered, as she'd told
Evan the first night they met. But the true
alchemy of wine came in the blending and
in the fermentation, in combining disparate
elements such as yeast and juice and adding
the passage of time. "In the end, St. Isadore
is just a place. I can take my skills with me
anywhere." She opened her eyes and peered
at Aracely. "Like, say, go to Chile with you?"

"You can travel wherever you want, whenever you want. Whether I'm going to Chile is

up for discussion." Aracely waved her hand. "But today we are packing. Where shall we start?"

"First, I'm starting with this red velvet cupcake. And then after…" Marguerite sighed again. "I guess the bedroom—"

A knock at the door downstairs caused Marguerite's and Aracely's heads to swivel as one in the direction of the sound.

"You're already here." Marguerite pointed out the obvious to Aracely. "Which means it must be…"

"Do you want me to answer the door?" Aracely asked.

Marguerite thought for a moment. The knocking came again, louder this time. She shook her head. "No. I may be leaving St. Isadore for good, but Napa will always be my home. And if Evan continues to own the winery, I'm bound to run into him either in town or at industry events. Might as well get it over with sooner rather than later."

And maybe, she thought to herself, maybe Evan had come to his senses faster than she'd thought possible. Maybe Evan was here to tell her she was right, and he was ready to let her in...

But it wasn't Evan on her doorstep. "Nico. Hi."

"Hey," Nico responded, tugging at the strap of the backpack he wore over one shoulder. "Do you have a few minutes?"

"Sure. And Aracely brought enough coffee and cupcakes to fuel an army, so you're in luck. Come in."

He closed the door behind him and trailed after her up the stairs. "First, I want you to remember that I'm just the messenger."

Marguerite waited until he was seated at the table with a chocolate-and-peanut-butter cupcake in front of him before she asked. "What message did Evan ask you to deliver? If it's about moving out of the carriage house, I'm way ahead of him."

"What? No," Nico exclaimed. "Unless you're moving out to live in the owner's residence."

Marguerite's gaze narrowed. "Evan sent you to ask me to move in with him? I doubt that."

"Sorry. No. Evan called me shortly after

sunrise, woke me up. Said he was leaving this morning for Asia. Something about saving a deal? Finding a new one? I wasn't very awake. But then he said he left some papers for you and asked me to deliver them." He opened up the backpack at his feet and took out a folder, then placed it on the table in front of Marguerite. "And I, um…" He shrugged.

Marguerite stared at the closed folder. "You read them."

"I peeked." Nico took a quick bite of his cupcake.

Marguerite pulled the folder toward her. And let it sit there.

"Well?" asked Aracely. "Are you going to open it or let me perish of suspense?"

Marguerite took a deep breath. She pulled back the cover of the file.

On top was a legal document. She picked it up and discovered it was a quitclaim deed, transferring ownership of St. Isadore to her. Evan's signature was bold in black, and he'd even found someone to notarize the document in what had to have been the middle of the night.

"And?" Aracely demanded.

Marguerite handed the deed to her, not sure she'd read it correctly. "I think… I think Evan gave St. Isadore to me."

Underneath the deed was Linus's will with her scrawled message on it. And below that was a copy of her employment contract, with a note attached in Evan's strong, confident script.

Marguerite,
Six months ago, we agreed we would revisit your contract after the Global Leader Summit. Congratulations, you've been promoted to owner of St. Isadore. You deserve it for your hard work, and it should have been yours all along. Never doubt how talented and capable you are.
Evan

She turned the pages of the contract. Evan had written "null and void" across each one. There were more papers in the folder, but they were a blur. She thought she had no more tears left after the night before. She was wrong.

Aracely gently removed the contract from

her hands and read through it. "There is also a financial overview and a phone number to call for access to St. Isadore's bank accounts and records. He left you enough cash to cover three years of operations."

Marguerite shook her head, slowly at first but then gathering momentum. "I can't accept this. Especially not—" she picked up the sheet Aracely referenced and blinked at the amount Evan had deposited into St. Isadore's coffers "—the money. Where did he say he was going?"

"He's on his way to Tokyo. Or maybe Shanghai?" Nico pondered. "He said something about Sydney, too, I think."

"Never mind. His office will know how to reach him." Marguerite gathered the papers together. "Neither of you say anything to anyone. I'll get this straightened out. Even if I have to climb Mt. Everest to find him."

"Good luck." Nico polished off the last of his cupcake. "Evan makes it extremely difficult to return his gifts. Ask me how I know."

"And what happens to St. Isadore in the meantime? Harvest is fast approaching. You,

of all people, know what a critical time period this is," Aracely pointed out.

"But Evan—" Marguerite squeezed her
eyes shut. "Evan needs St. Isadore or Angus
Horne won't invest."

"What?" Aracely sounded truly befuddled.

Nico paused in the midst of peeling the
wrapper off a second cupcake. "You don't
get it, do you, Marguerite? This is how Evan
shows you he cares. He gifts people things.
He's not going to take it back."

"I don't want 'things.' Even when the thing
is St. Isadore. I made that clear last night."

"I'm sure you did. But things are all Evan
gives. My grandparents used to say he took
the wrong lesson from our parents' death.
When he quit MIT to work full-time on his
first company, they wanted him to come
home and live with us in Boston. Be a family. Instead, he moved to Silicon Valley because, and I quote, 'Nico's not going to grow
up like I did.' He sent lots of money, but he
was too busy to visit."

Marguerite stared at Nico, her already-tat-
tered heart falling to pieces. "That's…awful.
Poor Evan."

"I thought maybe with you, he'd... Never mind." Nico took a bite and swallowed. "Meanwhile, Aracely is right about St. Isadore. Boss," he concluded with a smile.

"Regardless of who owns the winery, it is clear you are now in charge," Aracely added.

Marguerite regarded the papers, then shut the folder closed and shoved it away from her. "I'll talk to a lawyer on Monday. And if Evan changes his mind, he knows where I am. So for now, pass me a salted caramel cupcake."

She put a bright smile on her face and even managed to crack a few jokes as the three of them polished off the contents of the bakery box. But while she did her best to maintain a calm and even carefree facade, inside she began to shrivel, one molecule at a time.

For a very long while, owning even a part of St. Isadore had been her deepest desire. Now her lifelong dream had been handed to her on a diamond-encrusted, platinum platter. She should be ecstatic.

She would give it all up for one "I love you" from Evan's lips.

Maybe Nico was right. Maybe the deed was the closest thing to a declaration of affection she would get from Evan. Maybe it would be enough, ensuring her family's legacy would continue and under her direction.

Who knew attaining the goal she'd worked toward since childhood would be so devastating?

Eleven

Whoever said April was the cruelest month never met October. Or so it seemed to Evan, lugging his suitcase into an empty, cold house that smelled vaguely of cleaning products and little else. Of course, every month since last July had seemed cruel.

He'd mostly been away the last few months, chasing opportunities for Medevco in Asia or Europe, ever since he left St. Isadore for the last time. Nan kept his place in spotless order during his absences, but she could do nothing about the lack of warmth—and he didn't mean the heat from the furnace, which was doing its best to combat San Francisco's foggy, chilled night air. Once Marguerite had opened his eyes to his surroundings, he couldn't help but look at the rooms through her perspective. He'd made fun of St. Isadore's faux Victorian vibe, but he had to admit the overstuffed furniture and dozens of knickknacks scattered around gave it a lived-in, cared-for feeling that he only now realized was missing from this house.

House, not home.

By the time he unpacked and put his things back in their appropriate places, it was time for dinner. Or rather lunch, since he was still on Tokyo time. His housekeeper had left some casseroles in the refrigerator, but they required heating up, and besides, they were large enough to feed a family.

He didn't have a family.

He had his phone out and was about to order from his favorite takeout restaurant when his doorbell chimed. The security app showed a woman at his front door, her hair covered by a knit cap. His heart jumped while his stomach performed a somersault. Could it be…? Then, with a smile and a wave, the woman looked into the camera stationed over the door, and he could breathe easily again. "Hi, Danica," he said into the phone, knowing she would be able to hear him via the camera's speakers. "I'll buzz you in."

Evan had always liked Luke's wife. Blond and petite, she had a bubbly optimism that was the perfect complement to Luke's reserved practicality. Evan wasn't sure what she was doing at his place on a weeknight, however, especially since she and Luke lived forty-five minutes south in a tony enclave near Palo Alto. But he could guess. "I don't suppose you were just in the neighborhood and decided to stop by," he greeted her when she came in.

"No," Danica said, removing her hat and unbuttoning her coat, revealing a slightly rounded belly. "Although I am fond of the sushi restaurant at the bottom of your hill. Alas, no raw fish for me for the next several months."

"I see that. Congratulations. I had no idea you were…"

"Pregnant?" Danica raised her eyebrows. "Yes. I know you didn't know. Because Luke wanted to be the one to tell you, but you and Luke aren't talking except through memos."

Bingo. Evan's guess was correct. "I appreciate you coming all the way into the city. But this is a work matter. It'll be resolved eventually. Want something to drink before you return home? I have water—" he checked the refrigerator "—and water."

Danica followed him into the kitchen. "I'm not here because of Medevco. The company's future is between you and Luke—"

"And the board of directors," Evan muttered. In fact, he'd cut his latest business trip short after three weeks because of the emergency board meeting scheduled for tomorrow morning. And he still didn't have a replacement deal for the one he'd lost by turning down Angus Horne.

"Fine. And the board." Danica placed her hand on his arm. "I'm here as your friend who is concerned about you."

He choked on his sip of water. "Me? Why?"

"I get Luke can be bullheaded. I once didn't talk to him for about a month myself. But this current impasse between you is—"

She huffed and threw up her hands. "Luke showed me the numbers. Medevco will survive with or without the investment. It's in good health. But you're driving yourself into the ground chasing these deals. I'm afraid for *your* health."

"I'm fine." He picked up the basket of mail his housekeeper had left for him on the counter and started looking through it. Bills, appeals for donations, something from Pia he put aside to read later, renewal notices—

A dark purple envelope, embossed with the St. Isadore logo, with his name and address written in metallic-gold ink.

Danica must have heard his sharp intake of breath. "What's that?"

He shrugged, trying to appear nonchalant. But his pulse knocked against his eardrums. He hadn't spoken to Marguerite since their encounter in the library, although she appeared in his dreams both sleeping and waking. He did speak several times to his lawyers, ensuring his transfer of St. Isadore and its assets was as airtight as possible. Through them, he'd learned Marguerite had tried several times to have it invalidated and returned to him, but he'd held firm.

It was the least he could do.

Danica plucked the envelope from his fingers. "Oh! I know what this is. It's an invitation to the harvest dinner at St. Isadore. Luke and I received one."

He took the envelope back from her and shuffled it into the pile of mail discards. "Thanks. Now I don't need to open it."

"Evan." Danica's brows drew together.

"You're going to be a great mother. You have the I'm-so-disappointed-in-you tone down pat."

"I'm not disappointed. I'm concerned. Luke heard you gave the winery away, yet you're single-mindedly pursuing deals to grow Medevco beyond what is, frankly, reasonable." Her green gaze met his, soft with worry. "What's going on? This isn't like you."

Danica's concern was heartwarming, and that was the problem. He didn't want his heart warmed. He wanted it to remain neutrally cool, uninvolved. "I'm ensuring Medevco is a global success. Maybe becoming a father is making Luke too risk-averse."

Her gaze narrowed. "Okay. Pretend there's nothing driving your irrational behavior."

"Success isn't irrational."

"It is when you're destroying every relationship you have."

"Not if my actions keep the people in those relationships clothed and fed. Including you and Luke, in the case of Medevco."

She inhaled, then slowly let out her breath. "Do you think you're doing this for us? For the other people in your life? Evan, that's sweet. It's also condescending as hell."

"What?" Damn it, he didn't want to lose someone else from his life. But...

"You're treating us like inanimate figurines on a shelf, incapable of speaking on our own behalf, while you appoint yourself the sole arbiter of our welfare."

"No, I'm not. I'm—"

"Doing exactly that." She unfolded her arms and moved away from the counter, buttoning her coat as she went. "Y'know, Luke and I had high hopes that Marguerite—whom I like a lot, by the way—would open your eyes to the world beyond Medevco. But you gave away the winery, and in doing so, cut Marguerite out of your life, and now you're cutting Luke out by not speaking to him."

"That's not why I gave—" he sputtered.

She shook her head. "If you keep this up, Silicon Valley machinations are all you're going to have left. By yourself."

That had to be an empty threat. "Luke's not leaving Medevco."

She turned to face him. "Tomorrow? Of course not. And Luke makes his own decisions when it comes to business. I don't speak for him. But he won't put up forever with a partner who refuses to communicate." She yanked her knit cap over her blond curls. "Life is short, Evan. It's fine to spend it alone if that's what you truly want—but is it?"

She left without waiting for his answer, the front door closing behind her with a final-sounding click. Evan put down his nearly full glass of water to search for something stronger to drink.

Danica was wrong. He appreciated her loyalty to her husband, but she was wrong. Luke would come around once Evan secured the right deal. He just hadn't managed to find the best investor yet. And the only reason he gave away St. Isadore was because it wasn't his to keep.

The liquor cabinet was nearly empty. Maybe there was a forgotten beer in the refrigerator? But when he opened the door, a bottle of St. Isadore Chardonnay, chilling in the specialized beverage drawer, stared back at him. He started to close the door, only for his gaze to fall once more on the casseroles.

Casseroles, big enough to feed a family.

A vision of eating pizza at St. Isadore flashed through his head. Gabi laughing, Nico grinning as he snuck pieces of pepperoni off Evan's slices when he thought Evan wasn't looking, and Marguerite—

Marguerite smiling at him, her gaze filled with…

Love. Pure, sincere, true love.

Love for him.

Family had been there, all along, right under his nose. Love, his for the asking.

He shut his eyes. Screwed them tight. Tensed his muscles and steeled himself as the wave of regret, anguish and not a little anger at his willful blindness rolled over him.

Picking up his phone, he punched the button to call Danica's cell and then opened the invitation from St. Isadore. The harvest dinner was in a week. That might be enough time.

Danica answered over her car's sound system, street noise in the background. "I guess you're still speaking to me."

"I know you're driving, so I'll make this quick. I'm about to hop in my car and head down your way. Can you and Luke meet me in the bar at the Rosewood in an hour? I have a proposition for him, but you should weigh in."

There was a pause before Danica spoke. "Sure, as long as you buy me as many Shirley Temples as I want. See you then."

He hung up the phone, grabbed his coat and headed to his garage. Once again, he had a week. But this time he wasn't sure if he could pull off the miracle, or if he even deserved one. Still, he had to try.

Marguerite stood on the smooth flagstone terrace of St. Isadore, once more watching as guests began to arrive under the globe lights crisscrossing high overhead. Harvest was her favorite time of the year, and this harvest had been bountiful beyond her initial expectations. The grapes had been sorted and crushed and were fermenting in various tanks. Distributors were eager for the result, with restaurants as far away as Australia making inquiries about featuring her wines on their menus. Tonight was the culmination of dreams she'd spent a long time building. A celebration, in so many ways.

If only she felt like celebrating.

She accepted she was now the owner of St. Isadore. She'd tried various methods and ruses to reach Evan, to get him to recognize he had to take back his gift, but the lawyers were in agreement that the deed had been transferred to her, and Evan...

Well, Evan always sent very polite emails, but short to the point of being terse. And whenever she tried his cell phone, he'd seemed to be either on a plane or in a meeting.

Message received: he was avoiding her. If only her heart would take a clue and stop wanting him. But try as hard as she might, she couldn't convince herself she was wrong, that Evan didn't love her. She knew what she'd seen in his eyes that night in the library. But he wouldn't admit it, for whatever reason.

She was on track to repairing her family's legacy, but legacies did not keep her warm at night. Or make her laugh. Or challenge her. Or push her to be her best.

She'd read and reread his note, until the paper was in danger of falling apart where it was creased. She wanted to tell him that she no longer doubted herself. She yearned to tell him that she didn't doubt him or his love, either. If he would only give her the opportunity…

But that was something he had to realize by himself, for himself. She couldn't do it for him. In the meantime, there was delicious food to eat, exclusive wines to uncork and business to conduct. Evan had taught her about that, too. She geared herself up to go into the crowd—

And frowned. Aracely was running toward her. But Aracely didn't run. She ordinarily floated. "What's wrong?"

Aracely said something into the headset she wore, then turned to Marguerite. "Ted has to leave. He thinks something he ate at home did not agree with him."

"Oh, no." As director of operations, Ted was in charge of several key aspects of the harvest dinner. "Is he okay?"

Aracely nodded. "He will be fine. He tried to muscle through, but right now he's…" She wrinkled her nose. "Not something to discuss at a black-tie dinner people paid hundreds of dollars to attend."

"Poor Ted." Marguerite screwed her eyes shut to think. "Okay, I can take over—"

"But," Aracely interjected, "before he left, he called a friend and asked him to help out. Since we are short-staffed."

"We don't have time to train—"

"Ted gave him a quick quiz before he left, and he said his friend is well versed in St. Isadore's wines. But if you would like to talk to the friend, to make sure he is knowledge-able, Ted asked him to wait in the library."

"The library? Why not the winery office?"

"The winery is being used for VIP tours. This way, no one would see Ted…" Aracely mimed holding her stomach and groaning.

Marguerite narrowed her gaze. "I'm not

going to find Nico visiting from college, am I? This isn't some surprise you and he cooked up?"

Aracely's eyes widened. "Marguerite. I am shocked you would think that. The harvest dinner is the most important event of the year for St. Isadore. Would I pull you, the owner and winemaker, away from guests if this were not an emergency?" She folded her arms across her chest, the perfect picture of injured indignation.

Marguerite ran her gaze over the terrace. It was still early. The dinner itself wouldn't be served for another two hours. And if Ted was actually sick…and this mystery person could take on his duties…it would be a big assist. "Okay. I'll be back soon, with or without this person, depending on what he says."

But when Marguerite arrived in the library, it was empty. "Great," she muttered. Now she had someone she didn't know roaming the halls of the owner's residence while she needed to be with her guests. She huffed and turned to leave the room—

And stopped. The life-size portrait of Linus

was slightly askew, revealing darkness behind him. Someone had found the secret passage.

Her pulse quickened. Few people knew about the hidden hallways, and most of them weren't presently in residence at St. Isadore. Maybe someone from the cleaning staff had unlatched the door the last time they were in the library.

Then the floor rumbled below her feet. Surprised, she put out a hand to brace herself against the wall. What the—?

Of course. The elevator. The one that led to the owner's wine cellar.

She smiled. Was the room brighter, or was that only her vision, the dark filter that had hung over her since late July beginning to disappear as hope began to flood her senses? This could be a coincidence, she reminded herself, a simple malfunction of the elevator's wiring. It could be a real thief, using the cover of the party to steal the valuable rare wines. Or it could really be a friend of Ted's, doing some exploring while he waited.

There was one way to find out. She slipped

into the secret passage. But instead of following it to the elevator, she found the stairs. Kicking off her stiletto heels, she gathered the full skirt of her long, cobalt blue gown and descended to the cellar.

With a slight push, the door noiselessly glided open. She peeked around the edge.

The cellar lights were on, sconces of bronze and yellowed, frosted glass in an Art Deco fan shape that cast a diffuse, golden glow over the stone walls covered with racks of wine bottles. But her attention was caught by the man at the other end of the room, his black-clad back to her as he removed—

Wait. That was where she stored her experiments. She pushed the door all the way open. "Hey. That's *my* wine."

The man jumped. He almost dropped the bottle he was holding but managed to hold on to it. Then he slowly turned around.

Her breath caught. She knew who it would be, but she didn't know how glorious it would feel to be right. Evan. In a tuxedo. His smile slightly crooked, happy to see her but also a bit unsure.

"Aracely was supposed to give me fifteen more minutes," he said. "I'm not ready."

Her vision blurred and she blinked her eyes rapidly. She advanced into the room, barely noticing the cold stone floor against her bare feet. "Ready for what?"

He put the bottle down on the long wooden table in the middle of the cellar. "For my interview, of course."

"Your interview?" She wanted to smile. She wanted to do a thousand things: hug him, shake him, yell at him for avoiding her. Kiss him, now and forever. Instead, she indicated the wine. "But you're stealing my wine because…?"

He picked the bottle up again and regarded it, running the fingers of his other hand over the handwritten labeling. "I thought perhaps you might like a demonstration. Of my wine knowledge, that is."

She could no longer keep her smile buttoned down. It burst forth, stretching the corners of her mouth, digging deep into her cheeks. It was a full exhibit of the hopeful joy she allowed to bubble up. "Of course. I can't hire someone who doesn't appreciate wine.

But are you sure you want to open that one? It still has some aging to do."

"Oh, I don't have to open it." He moved closer to her. "I already know it's spectacular. Complex. Assertive. Unpredictable at times. Full of rich, vivid notes that only deepen with longer acquaintance. A presence that can't be forgotten, even if you try. A wine worth fighting for."

She started to laugh. "You know all this without even opening the bottle?"

He nodded. "I know the maker. She puts herself into everything she does."

Her laughter died in her throat, replaced by a thick ball of emotion making it hard to swallow. Her nose burned, a sure sign more tears were on their way, but she forced them back. "There's one problem. You already have a job. A big one."

He shook his head. And then he came even closer. "I no longer work for Medevco. I turned over sole control to Luke. The board approved the change a few days ago."

Was the cellar spinning around her? Or maybe it was the effect of losing herself in Evan's kaleidoscopic gaze. "I don't— What?"

He reached out, and now her hands were in his. "You're freezing," he said, rubbing her fingers, wrapping his hands around hers.

"I'm okay." She did tremble but not from the temperature in the room.

Evan frowned. "Maybe we should leave the cellar."

If they left, they would be surrounded by staff and guests. She would be swept up in the bustle of the dinner. Down here, they were alone, in their own world. "Tell me now. Why did you sell to Luke?"

His gaze was focused on her feet. She pulled her bare toes under her gown but not before he noted them. He gave her a decisive nod. Then, with one sweeping motion he picked her up, pulling her onto his lap as he sat on the table.

"Evan." She wriggled to get down, then realized that perhaps it wasn't the most prudent movement. Not right now.

"You want to hear the story, I don't want you to expire of cold before I'm done."

"Fine. Speak." Truth to tell, she didn't want to be anywhere else but nestled against his warmth, surrounded by the Evan-scent she'd doubted she would ever experience again.

"You were right." His words rumbled in her ear.

"About? Although I do love it when people admit that."

Evan's arms tightened around her. "Never doubt your talents. Or how perceptive you are."

"Have you forgiven yourself for whatever it was?" she asked quietly.

He stilled, only his chest rising and falling against her. "How did you know there was something to forgive?"

"Nico said something, the morning you gave me St. Isadore. About how angry your grandparents were with you."

He shifted, and she moved to leave his lap, thinking perhaps she was too heavy, but he kept her tight against him. "If you don't want to talk about it, that's okay," she said.

Only the sounds of their breathing interrupted the stillness. "I never wanted a family," he finally said. "I didn't want to leave anyone behind like I was left. Like Nico was left."

She squeezed her eyes shut, hurting for the young Evan. "I understand."

"My dad—my dad and mom were coming home after dropping me at MIT for my sophomore year. He'd taken a second job. I don't remember now what it was. Something that kept him up all night after a long day in the auto shop. The police thought…they thought he fell asleep. He drifted into another lane and never saw the oncoming truck."

"I'm so sorry," she whispered, her lips against his cheek.

"I kept thinking if he didn't take that second job, they'd still be here. Nico would've grown up knowing them."

"You drove yourself so no one else would have to worry about extra income," she guessed. "That's why you bought St. Isadore. That's why you wanted Medevco to grow so fast. So Nico wouldn't want for anything."

"Told you you're perceptive."

"Did you give me St. Isadore for the same reason? So I'd be taken care of?"

He didn't answer.

She slid out of his grasp, ignoring his muttered protest, and turned to face him. He remained seated on the table, which allowed their gazes to be level. "Evan. I'll ask you the same question you asked me that night we first met. Why are you here?"

He shrugged, his half grin reappearing. "I have it on good authority my drive was hurting, not helping Medevco. So I left, which means I'm jobless. You're the boss now, so I thought I'd throw myself on your mercy."

Inside, she was smiling so hard her cheeks hurt. But she managed to keep a straight expression. "Then, this is a job interview. What skills will you bring to St. Isadore? I run a lean operation, you know."

He thought for a moment. "We discussed how I'm a hard worker. I'm punctual. And I'm a fast learner."

She nodded. "Those are all admirable qualities. But I'm afraid we have no openings right now."

"I thought you might say that, so I took the liberty of coming up with my own job description."

"Really?" It was harder and harder to control her expression, so she stopped trying. Joy began to spill from every pore. "Part-time or full time?"

"Definitely full time." He jumped off the

table. Her gaze followed him as he went to the section of the cellar where sparkling wines were stored. He selected a bottle and came back.

She recognized the label. "That's definitely the good stuff."

"If I don't get the job, I promise I'll replace it." He removed the foil, exposing the cork and the wire cage keeping it in place. "Did you know," he said conversationally as he turned the key to loosen the cage, "that this always takes six twists?"

She nodded. "Of course."

"But do you know the legend why?" He removed the cage, twisting it into some shape she couldn't see. Then he dropped to one knee.

She gasped. The tears that had been threatening all night breached the defenses and flowed, unchecked, down her cheeks. Her entire being trembled, and it definitely had nothing to do with being cold.

"Six is the number of extreme happiness, or so I was assured by my local wine-store owner. And while that may only be a tall tale when it comes to champagne, I know it is the absolute truth when I'm with you. You asked me why I'm here. I'm hoping you will forgive me and allow me to serve as your husband." He held out the wire cage, twisted into the shape of a ring with the cork cap serving as the stone. "I love you, Daisy Marguerite Delacroix. You stole my heart from the moment we met."

"Evan." She clapped her hands over her mouth, unable to speak, unable to move, unsure if this moment—so often dreamed of—was truly real.

His smile faltered. "I'd settle for committed boyfriend if you require a probationary period first?"

She shook her head and tugged him up, allowing him to slip the twisted wire onto the fourth finger of her left hand, her heart still too full for her brain to form words.

"This was supposed to happen in the library," he said. "There's a real ring in the desk drawer."

Finally, she found words. Just a few. "This is perfect. Yes. A thousand times yes."

Then he was kissing her and she was kissing him and the cellar spun around them until she was dizzy with love and happiness and hope. They might have stayed down there until the cleaning crew arrived the next day if Aracely hadn't poked her head into the room.

"Why do I always find discarded articles of clothing when you two are together?" she asked, holding up Marguerite's forgotten shoes. "I am so sorry to interrupt—"

"We're sorry to interrupt," said a grinning Nico, appearing from behind Aracely.

"But there is a dinner going on—" Aracely finished.

"Which I don't want to miss since I'm only in town tonight to hang out with my brother. And you of course, Marguerite," Nico interjected.

"And the presence of the owner is requested," Aracely finished.

"That's you," Evan whispered against her lips. "I couldn't be prouder of everything you've accomplished."

"St. Isadore is a group effort." She ran her fingers over his lightly stubbled cheeks, still amazed he was here, in her arms. "You're a part of it. If you want to be."

"All I want is you," he said. "Today, tomorrow and to infinity. But I'd be thrilled to be on your team. Whatever you want. After all, you're the boss now." He grinned, that devilish, cocky grin that made her heart take flight and soar into the heavens.

"Whatever we want," she corrected, and took his hand to lead him out of the cellar, following Aracely and Nico up to the terrace to join the festivities. There was more to celebrate than she had dreamed would be possible. "Together."

* * * * *